WEDDING *Her* *Christmas* DUKE

SEDUCTIVE SCOUNDRELS, BOOK TEN

COLLETTE CAMERON

Blue Rose Romance®

Sweet-to-Spicy Timeless Romance®

"I canna just let ye go."

Baxter pressed his mouth to the crown of her head.

"I dinna ken what this is between us,

but I've never felt anythin' like it, Justina."

Other Collette Cameron Books

Check out Collette's Other Series
Daughters of Desire (Scandalous Ladies)
Highland Heather Romancing a Scot
The Blue Rose Regency Romances:
The Culpepper Misses
Castle Brides
The Honorable Rogues®
Heart of a Scot

Collections
Lords in Love
Heart of a Scot Books 1-3
The Honorable Rogues® Books 1-3
The Honorable Rogues® Books 4-6
Seductive Scoundrels Series Books 1-3
Seductive Scoundrels Series Books 4-6
The Blue Rose Regency Romances-
The Culpepper Misses Series 1-2

Dedication

Hoping your Christmas is magical and romantic.

Many blessings to you this holiday season

and throughout the rest of the year too.

Bathhurst Hotel and Spa
Bath, Somerset, England
15 November 1810

Justina Farthington laughed as she and her widowed aunt, Emily Grenville, tried in vain to dodge the large, soggy snowflakes sifting from the pewter gray sky with the rambunctious abandon of a litter of kittens playing in a sack of spilled flour. The pathway to the hotel wasn't long, but the snow made walking difficult.

"It's a good thing we didn't plan on reaching home today," Justina said, tilting her head to better study the ominous sky. A plump snowflake plopped onto her chin, and she laughed again. Grateful for her warm leather gloves, she swiped the moisture away. "We'd never have made it to Bristol in this weather."

"In all of my years, I have never known it to snow this heavily in Somerset in November," Aunt Emily declared, clutching Justina's hand for balance.

A good five inches of snow had already accumulated. Though it was scarcely an hour past one in the afternoon, steel gray blanketed the town so popular with the upper ten thousand, giving the appearance of early twilight. The pouting sky showed no signs of relenting in its unrepentant white onslaught upon the earth either.

Surely snow in Somerset wasn't so scarce.

"Yes, all *thirty* of your years," Justina remarked dryly while concentrating on keeping snow from sneaking into her half-boots. "And because you're *so* well-traveled."

"Hush, Justina Madalene Honoria Farthington. *Really.* Reminding me of my advanced age and that I'm on the shelf is beyond the pale," Emily huffed good-naturedly, even as a frown puckered her brow.

Oh, my heavens. Auntie used my full name. She is

in a fine fettle, then.

"Lest you forget, I am widowed and a decade your senior. And, I'll remind you, dear niece, that I have seen much more of this often-unforgiving world than you."

"Of course, forgive me for suggesting otherwise," Justina murmured demurely.

Aunt Emily wasn't done, however.

"You know full well I accompanied my brother on his diplomatic jaunts for several years. It simply does not snow several inches before Christmastide in our part of the world."

A touch of genuine concern had leeched into Aunt Emily's usually tranquil tones.

Was her aunt worried they'd be stranded here?

What did it matter?

Their finances, though not abundant, were sufficient to accommodate an extended stay. No one awaited them at home in Bristol, except two doddering servants, well past their prime. And the Sutcliffes' Christmastide house party didn't begin until the twenty-second of December—a full month away.

In point of fact, Justina and her aunt were invited to come a few days prior. Nonetheless, they could while away for a fortnight in Bath, and no one would be the wiser, much less worried or concerned.

A grin played around the edges of Justina's mouth.

Oh, how she looked forward to the Sutcliffes' house party.

Her dearest friends—young women she'd met at the finishing school her widowed aunt had insisted she attend—were also invited. Genuine excitement that today's gloomy weather and the disruption to their travel plans couldn't diminish bubbled along her veins.

Clutching Justina's hand tighter, Aunt Emily clicked her tongue, reminding Justina very much of their elderly neighbor, Gertrude Howerton.

Nearly blind and well on her way to becoming deaf as well, Gertrude was forever fussing over something, *tsking*, clucking, and murmuring, "Mercy," or "God save me," while forcefully pounding her cane on whatever unfortunate surface she happened to be upon, or prodding the legs of whoever happened to be in proximity of the flailing stick.

She was precisely the type of eccentric old bird Justina hoped she'd be in her dotage.

Though still a beautiful woman, Aunt Emily dressed and acted like a seventy-year-old spinster. If a man so much as gave her a second glance, with her lips pursed, she turned her frostiest green-eyed stare upon him. Usually, that was sufficient to send any would-be swains trotting hastily in the other direction.

She never—*truly never*—spoke of her marriage or dead husband, an officer in His Majesty's Navy. Once that first year together, struggling to find the right words in her stilted English, Justina had dared ask Emily about her husband.

Distress had ravaged her aunt's pretty features before she'd managed, "It is not something I ever speak of."

Justina had never poked her nose into Aunt Emily's personal business again. Somehow, she sensed it wasn't just grief that tied her aunt's tongue and caused the haunted shadows in her pretty eyes.

"It is most unfortunate that the Royal Arms Hotel

suffered fire damage, and we are obliged to find lodgings elsewhere." Aunt Emily signaled the drivers to wait. "Richard always insisted we stay at the Royal Arms."

In truth, this was the third establishment the women had stopped at, seeking rooms for the night. Who would've guessed so many dratted people were traveling in November despite the awful roads?

With a wan smile, Aunt Emily allowed, "My brother was rather rigid and unyielding in his ways. A deeply devout man, Richard never stepped over the mark or outside Society's strictures."

Justina kept her less than charitable response to herself.

Whenever Aunt Emily mentioned Richard Farthington, Justina couldn't prevent her heart from cramping. Not over his death, for she hadn't known the man, but for all the ugliness that had come afterward.

Could he really have been gone nearly a decade?

How well she remembered that day less than a month before her tenth birthday. The day after her beloved mother had died in their humble Viennese hovel and her cantankerous Austrian grandfather had presented Justina at Richard Farthington's doorstep, proclaiming she was his illegitimate daughter.

"I've no use for a *uneheliches Kind*" —bastard child— "under my feet," grandfather had pronounced coldly in his German spattered, halting English. "Farthington impregnated my daughter, and he can deal with *das Mädchen* now that my Elsa is gone, *ja*?"

He hadn't even looked back but had left Justina standing bereft and teary-eyed with an equally confused and grief-stricken Emily Grenville. She'd buried her brother, Richard, a mere two days before, after he'd succumbed to lung fever.

Except for each other, Justina and Aunt Emily were indeed two women alone in the world.

As always, when reminiscing about her previous life, melancholy infused Justina.

She cut a sideways glance at the woman who'd become mother, sister, and friend to her in the ensuing years. The woman who'd accepted a child she neither knew nor could vouch for her paternity and brought that same frightened and sad little girl to England to be raised as a gentle-woman. The only person—save Wenzel Trattner, Justina's grandfather—who knew the secret of her birth and guarded it like the most precious of gems.

Aunt Emily had, however, changed Justina's given name from Friederike, giving her a feminine version of Richard Farthington's middle name, Justin. For that, Justina was grateful. Simply put, Friederike was a mouthful, and she would have had to continually explain her name's origin had she kept it.

Although, in retrospect, she might've enjoyed being called Freddie.

The great-granddaughter of a viscount, Emily Grenville, had taken a grief-stricken child beneath her wing that awful afternoon when the charcoal grey Vienna sky had also been cloaked with grumpy clouds.

A few years later, Justina had learned that Emily's branch of the family had long ago spurned contact with the distant relations they had peppered about England and beyond. No reason was given for the estrangement.

Shorter than Justina, at just two inches above five

feet, and older than her by ten years, Emily was the opposite of Justina in almost every way, except for the green eyes they shared.

Justina's were a pale green, while Emily's were darker jade. The eye color did not signify paternity, as they both well knew. But it did aid in strengthening the fabricated tale Aunt Emily had concocted that long-ago day. Thus far, no one had questioned the story. It contained just enough scandal to titillate and a thread of truth that could neither be proven nor disproven.

To the world, Justina was Richard Farthington's daughter. His Viennese wife, Justina's mother, had died in childbirth.

End of story.

Only it wasn't.

For one thing, Justina and Aunt Emily, save for their eyes, looked nothing alike.

Aunt Emily was golden-haired, possessed of a keen wit, and pragmatic to the point of causing Justina to grind her teeth on occasion. She possessed an oval face, winged eyebrows, and though not precisely beautiful in the traditional sense, she attracted men like plump blossoms did bees in the summertime.

She'd received a half dozen marriage proposals since putting aside her mourning weeds. All of which she'd declined with the alacrity of a starving urchin stealing a sweetmeat from a baker.

Emily Grenville was determined to never—*ever*— marry again. Something that Justina was just as determined to thwart. For, truth be told, if anyone deserved love, companionship, and children, it was her unselfish aunt.

Justina, on the other hand, possessed straight light brown hair, a diamond-shaped face with a chin she thought much too pointed, and eyebrows that refused to arch no matter how studiously she plucked the dashed things. Her curves, especially her breasts, were abundant compared to Emily's gentle swells.

Although Aunt Emily argued otherwise, Justina felt certain her aunt had rejected those marriage offers because she refused to sequester Justina at a country house and go on with her life.

When she'd taken on the responsibility of Justina's care, she'd scarcely been twenty years old herself. Fourteen years younger than Richard Farthington, after their parents had died, Emily had acted as her brother's hostess for five of those years.

Well, except for the two months she'd been married.

Two months—then tragically widowed.

What had scarred Aunt Emily so that she avoided any mention of her marriage or her husband, Lieutenant Clement Grenville?

Someday, Justina would know the truth.

In any event, Aunt Emily had been her brother's sole heir.

Prudently managed—and Emily was nothing if not prudent—his bequeathment had proven sufficient to support the two women in relative comfort as long as they practiced economies. Theirs was not a luxurious lifestyle by any means, but they needn't be ashamed of their social standing either.

Farther down the lane, children squealed and ran about pelting each other with snowballs or pulling one another along on sleds. A wonder they even owned sleds, so infrequent was snow here.

A black dog yapped, its tail wagging furiously as it chased after the snowballs. Three industrious boys were intent on building a snowman while two little girls lay upon their backs making snow angels.

There'd be many cold noses, fingers, and toes, and no doubt hot chocolate or perhaps mulled wine to chase away the chill this afternoon. In truth, at the moment, a hot toddy sounded utterly divine.

An unwelcome memory pushed to the forefront of Justina's mind: a petite girl in a pale blue cloak laying on her back and making a snow angel.

As quickly as the recollection had intruded, it vanished.

She'd been that little girl. But as with the other memories of her former life, that vision swirled around the edges of her memory before floating away. Try as she might, she could no longer summon the image of her mother's face but remembered her kind blue eyes and her pretty voice as she sang to Justina.

She and her aunt tramped up the four steps to Bathhurst Hotel and Spa and stomped their snow-caked half-boots upon the colorful braided rug outside the door.

Somewhere within, a dog woofed a canine greeting.

A small frown forming two lines on her forehead, Emily squinted at the newly painted sign and then slowly took in the welcoming porch.

"I think the hotel has recently been painted and refurbished." She pointed at the sign. "And renamed, as well. It was simply *The Bath House* the last time I was in Bath."

When?

A decade ago?

Or longer?

Justina took in the dark green script announcing the establishment's name as well as the well-appointed porch upon which sat several rocking chairs, a porch swing, and two benches. All contained cushions and thick throws for those guests bold enough to brave the outdoors in November.

Aunt Emily brushed the snow from the shoulders of her wren-brown redingote, then raised her black-gloved fist to knock upon the door, painted the same vibrant green as the sign. However, before she rapped, the carved panel swung inward, revealing a footman attired in neat green and black livery.

A black patch covered his left eye, and a wicked-looking scar creased his cheek and jaw.

A former soldier?

"I think the new owner has a penchant for green," Justina whispered out the side of her mouth.

The footman's lips twitched, and his good eye, a warm and friendly pale brown, twinkled in merriment. "Indeed, he does admire the shade a great deal. Wait until you see the dining room and the greenhouse. All manner of exotic birds are housed there, every one of them rescued in one manner or another."

Ah, so the man has a tender heart.

Pride evident in his voice and bearing, the servant declared, "Mr. Bathhurst is quite the philanthropist."

Bathhurst?

The man was vain enough to name the establishment after himself. Certainly not unusual, but it did give one pause.

As if reading Justina's thoughts, Aunt Emily

queried, "Bathhurst?" She tapped the small dimple in her chin. "The name is familiar, though I cannot think why. Perhaps he is an acquaintance of one of our ducal friends."

Aunt Emily referred to several of Justina's school friends, six of which were now married to dukes.

Extraordinary.

Duchesses, each and every one, and not all nobly born themselves.

But none were born on the wrong side of the blanket, either.

Justina stepped inside, taking in the polished parquet flooring and a pair of matching tufted benches on either side of the foyer. These were seafoam green, rather than the emerald hue of the front door. A marble-topped rosewood table flanked each bench, and at the far end of the entrance, a pair of highbacked chairs—not green, but claret-colored—drew one's attention to another table upon which appeared to be a chess set.

Clearly, the entry was intended to be used for more than guests entering and exiting the establishment. It felt homey and hospitable, the furnishings tasteful and understated but of unmistakable quality.

A scraggly dog in mottled shades of black, brown, and gray and favoring his front left paw emerged from a room farther along the corridor and lifted its nose, sniffing the air. Evidently satisfied Justina and her aunt were not a threat, he lumbered forward, his gait uneven.

He plopped on his haunches beside Justina, gazing at her expectantly, and she ran a hand over his soft head. He whimpered and rested his head against her leg, staring at her adoringly.

The flirt. Did the little beggar hope to get more pets?

"Do you have any rooms available?" Aunt Emily asked without preamble.

Her aunt's inquiry snapped Justina back to the present, and she offered a hopeful smile.

Good gracious, what were they to do if Bathhurst Hotel and Spa were full as well? Many of the hotels had closed for the off-season, and she'd considered them fortunate that this lodging house was open so near the main route to Bristol.

"Indeed, we do, ladies." The footman nodded in the affirmative as another joined him.

This one boasted a distinct limp, and upon further covert inspection, Justina realized he was missing two fingers on his right hand.

Yes, most definitely a former soldier.

Her opinion of Mr. Bathhurst rose another notch.

Many employers wouldn't hire those maimed by war, and yet not only did Mr. Bathhurst rescue birds, of all things, but he also gave positions to those most in need.

"We'll see to your bags. You can check in there." The second footman angled his head toward a gleaming mahogany counter, paralleling a staircase to the upper floors. "I am Coyle, and this is Perkins." He indicated the first footman. "Oh, and the dog's name is Duke. Mr. Bathhurst has a sardonic sense of humor."

Indeed, he did, for Justina had never seen a less aristocratic appearing canine in her entire life.

Duke, indeed.

"Welcome, to Bathhurst Hotel and Spa," a wiry little man wearing spectacles boomed from beside the gleaming counter. "We just finished updating and refurbishing the hotel."

Justina started at the commanding voice coming from such a diminutive man. He couldn't have been above four feet in stature, and she realized he must be a dwarf. Behind his spectacled eyes, lively intelligence and humor shone. Liking him at once, she returned his congenial smile.

"I am Solomon Bixby, manager of this fine establishment," he announced, pride ringing in his unique voice. "You've arrived in time for afternoon tea in the drawing room, ladies. We've six other guests presently staying with us," he added, almost as an afterthought. "We'll see that the fires are stoked in your chambers, and they'll be warm as bread fresh from the oven in no time."

"Thank you, Mr. Bixby. That sounds simply wonderful." As she usually did, Emily took charge.

Of late, that habit had begun to grate on Justina a bit. She was far more capable than her overly-protective aunt allowed. Others had noticed Emily's protectiveness too. Why, at the Twistleton's musical last March, she'd overheard two nobles referring to Aunt Emily as a dragon.

Affront for the woman she'd called aunt for a decade encompassed Justina.

Aunt Emily was nothing like an angry, violent, intimidating dragon. She was simply cautious and guarded. A young widow having a ward thrust upon her and having to navigate Society without raising suspicion wasn't easy.

Keeping the secret they both well knew could destroy them wasn't easy either.

2

Bathhurst Hotel and Spa

An hour later

Baxter Bathhurst threw open the back door, his preferred entrance, to the hotel. Stepping aside to allow Princess to bolt inside and find her injured brother, he balanced the box containing the honey he'd purchased this afternoon.

He raised his head slightly and sniffed appreciatively.

Mmm.

Roast beef for supper tonight, and—Baxter inhaled again, turning his mouth upward into a satisfied smile—apple pie if he weren't mistaken.

"Nothin' like a slice of pie to warm a mon's body," he muttered to himself, allowing the Scot's brogue he usually kept in check to roll off his tongue.

It grated the English's pompous arses that he, the son of a simple Scottish innkeeper and tavern owner, should've inherited the elite San Sebastian dukedom. A smirk pulling his mouth to the side, Baxter shook his head, still reluctant to believe he was a sodding duke— had been for five bloody years now.

This was the world he preferred.

The life he'd enjoyed for his first five-and-twenty years. The simple, fulfilling existence of a hotelier. Well, he owned six hotels now, in addition to several other businesses, but never mind that. He'd used his title and influence to help the less fortunate by hiring those others wouldn't employ.

The world was a cruel, cold, heartless place to anyone deemed *different.*

He didn't even permit his staff, who were aware he was titled, to address him as San Sebastian or Your Grace. *That* personage was reserved for London or, at the very least, assemblies and the like, which required him to acknowledge his English birthright.

He grimaced upon recollecting he was expected in London in a fortnight, and he'd foolishly allowed the dukes of Heatherton, Pennington, and Bainbridge to coax him into attending the Duke and Duchess of Sutcliffes' Christmastide house party.

God curse my three-times great grandfather for not having more older sons.

God curse *me* for a fool.

Setting the box on the table provided for just such articles, Baxter nudged the door closed with his boot heel. As it clicked shut with a satisfying *snick*, he shucked his caped greatcoat. After hanging it on a hook, he removed his hat, scarf, and gloves. They landed in a heap next to the box of honey.

Finally, with a shake of his head to dislodge any lingering snowflakes, he picked up the honey and marched down the wooden corridor to the kitchen. Mrs. Felton would be beside herself when she saw the treasure he carried, and Baxter could count on fresh rolls liberally topped with butter and honey for several days to come.

As he entered the kitchen, Mrs. Felton glanced up from arranging biscuits and other dainties on a tray.

"Just in time, Mr. Bathhurst. Coyle is taking another tray to our guests, momentarily. We've eight now, and the cold seems to have stimulated their appetites."

Brisk weather had a way of doing that.

He supposed humans weren't any different than other species that fattened up in preparation for a long, cold winter.

Baxter set the honey down on the table and gestured. "I persuaded that crusty old bugger, Warner, to part with a dozen jars of honey."

In truth, the old man had been in dire need of finances but was too proud to accept charity. Baxter had paid five times what the honey was worth and would've paid double that. He also meant to see Warner's roof was repaired and that he had sufficient wood to last him the winter. And that his beehives provided honey for Baxter's five other hotels, three restaurants, and his signature mead.

"Oh, my!" Mrs. Felton's face lit up, and she

promptly brushed her hands together to rid them of crumbs before wiping them on a damp cloth.

Enjoying her excitement, he chuckled.

"Such a treat," she said, making her way to the table, a smudge of flour on her dark brown cheek. Black eyes shining, she picked up a jar of the amber liquid and winked. "I suppose you'll want fresh oatmeal rolls to go with supper tonight?"

Baxter gave her a boyish grin. "If it wouldn't be too much trouble."

"Go on with you. Greet your guests and have a cup of strong tea," she said in her lyrical voice as she motioned toward the door leading to the main house. "I'll make enough rolls to keep you satisfied for a few days."

"Thank ye." The rolls reminded Baxter of his homeland.

He might be an English duke, but his heart would always belong to Scotland.

Hesitating for an instant, he pondered whether he ought to make himself presentable first. Glancing down, he noted the melting snow on his Hessians, but other than that, he looked presentable enough in his fine black wool jacket and trousers, he supposed.

After all, this wasn't Almack's Assembly Rooms or Countess Lieven's drawing room.

He'd never been one to put on airs or wear fancy togs. What was good for the ordinary folks was suitable for him too. Having made his decision, Baxter gave Mrs. Felton a jaunty wave and wink before turning and following the meandering corridor toward the main part of the hotel.

As he walked, voices carried to him marked by an occasional laugh.

He slowly curved his mouth upward into a lazy smile.

Excellent.

If his guests were pleased, they'd spread the word, and in turn, more guests would visit the hotel. As with his other establishments, once Bathhurst Hotel and Spa was running efficiently and profitably, he'd turn the management of the hotel and spa over to a trusted servant. In this case, Solomon Bixby, and then Baxter would move on to his next project, which he'd yet to identify.

Another hotel? A restaurant?

No, he wished to try his hand at something different this time.

But what?

Horse breeding? Shipping? Investments in new inventions?

Now there was an intriguing notion.

Humankind was capable of such extraordinary ingenuity.

A life of idleness and boredom, filling his days with walks and rides in Hyde Park, attending a mind-numbing series of balls, routs, and soirees, or gambling, drinking, and wenching were not for him. Even if he was a bloody duke.

Baxter made a discontented noise in the back of his throat.

Glancing at himself in a gilded mirror above a highly polished table, he stopped short. His thick, dark blond hair needed brushing. Instead, he raked his fingers through the unruly tresses a few times, managing to tame the worst of his mane.

He stared back at the man in the reflection. The pale brown eyes—very near the color of the honey in the kitchen—gazed back at him: his mother's eyes and hair rather than his sire's black hair and piercing blue eyes.

As he'd never wanted for feminine company when he desired it, Baxter supposed he was attractive enough. However, now that he'd come into a title, he never knew whether a woman was genuinely interested in him or if the dukedom posed the attraction.

More on point, he didn't know if becoming the next Duchess of San Sebastian motivated the eager women flocking to his side.

With a careless shrug, he continued on his way.

Unless he mastered mind-reading—which was as likely as sprouting wings or a second head—he could never be certain of any woman's motives.

At the entrance to the drawing room, Baxter took a moment to assess his guests.

Mildred and Marian Popkin, an elderly pair of spinster sisters, perched like a pair of curious birds on the edge of a forest green settee. They batted their almost nonexistent eyelashes behind their matching spectacles at Mister Godfrey Howlette, a self-important dandy standing by the fireplace, posing for the benefit of the ladies.

Obnoxious coxcomb.

Baxter almost expected him to stretch out his neck and crow, so obvious was his posturing.

Paul and Hester Harmon occupied the armchairs nestled in the bay window. Newlyweds, they only had eyes for each other, though each did glance in Baxter's direction and gave a brief nod in greeting.

Of middling years and boasting quite the most astonishing mutton chops Baxter had ever seen, Major Carlton Spaulding of His Majesty's Army conversed with the new arrivals, both of whom had their backs to the entry.

Miss Mildred spied Baxter first and fluttered her fan flirtatiously. It somewhat resembled an angry or startled fowl flapping his wings. "Mr. Bathhurst. Please do join us and permit us—

"—to introduce Mrs. Grenville and her niece, Miss Farthington, to you," her sister finished in a rush.

Every person in the room turned their attention to Baxter as he sauntered into the drawing room. When he bowed, his gaze meshed with the younger woman with eyes the color of the filmy ferns and horsetails growing in the damp woods near Strathyre.

Ah, green. My favorite color.

His signature color too. Which was why all of his establishments were decorated with a matching theme: shades of greens and burgundies.

He found himself staring, and pink tinted the young woman's high cheekbones before midnight lashes lowered to fan her cheeks, and she turned her head away.

Coyle arrived with the promised tray, and Baxter gave a silent prayer of thanks for the interruption. Else he would still gawp like a farmhand seeing a proper lady for the first time.

He bowed, perhaps more extravagantly than needed. "Ladies and gentlemen, our fondest wish at Bathhurst Hotel and Spa is to meet your every need. Should you require anything, we'll do our utmost to provide it for you."

He didn't miss the sly, lecherous gaze Howlette slid the pretty woman from beneath his half-closed eyes.

Scunner.

Baxter forced his hands to relax at his sides rather than curl into fists. And punch the lecherous glint from the dandy's face. Clearing his throat, Baxter produced one of his most amiable smiles.

"Anything within the strictures of propriety, that is, of course."

An ugly flush washed Howlette's face, and Baxter swore the green-eyed goddess hid a grin behind her fan. Humor assuredly sparkled in her eyes.

Major Spaulding abruptly coughed into his tea, which caused both of the Popkin sisters to fuss and declare they hoped he wasn't coming down with the ague.

In short order, introductions were made, and Baxter had claimed a seat beside Miss Marian. No sense in being too obvious, even if Miss Farthington had captured his interest the moment their eyes had met. However, he couldn't prevent his attention from straying to her several times.

Her hawk-eyed aunt caught his perusal and arched one winged eyebrow knowingly. Her keen gaze seemed to say, *"Caught you, cad."*

"So, what brings you to Bath during the first snowstorm in a decade, Mrs. Grenville?" Baxter asked conversationally when what he really wanted to do was ask the niece where she'd been all of his life.

A pretty blonde, either late in her third decade or early in her fourth, she regarded him for a long moment before answering smoothly.

"My niece and I are en route to our home. The roads were simply too unmanageable, and I feared for the safety of our drivers and the team. Generally, when in this area, we stay at the Royal Arms. However, as I'm sure you know, they suffered a fire recently. Therefore, we sought lodgings elsewhere. We'll be on our way as soon as this unfavorable weather allows."

"I'm certain your drivers will be satisfied with their accommodations in the stables," Baxter said. His confidence was well-placed since he'd assured the servants' quarters at Bathhurst Hotel and Spa were clean and comfortable.

He didn't fail to notice Mrs. Grenville hadn't mentioned precisely where their home was. He couldn't decide if he admired her for her protectiveness or if her ambiguity irked him. Nor could he help but wonder if her attitude would rapidly change if she knew he was, in fact, a duke.

Most people turned into simpering sycophants, and it annoyed the very devil out of him.

"Most fortunate for us," Major Spaulding offered. Having recovered from his fit of coughing, he puffed out his barrel-like chest. "Do either of you play cards?" he asked hopefully.

The Major was a terrible cheat, and the Popkin sisters equally dreadful players.

Both sisters speared him an injured look. Their numbers had been balanced until the arrival of today's guests, and even if Baxter took part in the evening's entertainment, they were one male short. Which meant someone would always be the extra wheel.

"Indeed, Major," Miss Farthington answered as she lifted her cup to those pink, bowed lips and blew gently on the piping hot tea she'd just poured herself. "I prefer whist or vingt-et-un, but my aunt is quite accomplished at piquet and is simply brilliant on the pianoforte."

None of Baxter's current guests had shown any interest in playing the instrument.

Howlette gazed around the room, a rather cunning glint in his eye. Pulling on the lapels of his bright blue jacket, he said, "I say, why don't we have dancing after dinner tonight?"

Even the newlyweds perked up at that suggestion.

"What a splendid idea," Mrs. Harmon said, catching her husband's hand in hers.

"Oh, we quite adore dancing," gushed Miss Marian. "Do we not, Sister?"

Her sister bobbed her head, the purple feather tucked into her steel-gray coiffure gyrating at the movement.

"Indeed, we do," she agreed, peering at Mrs. Grenville expectantly.

The Popkin sisters' fans fluttered so vigorously that Baxter pondered if they might become airborne in their enthusiasm.

"Ah, but our new guests have only just arrived, and they might wish to retire early this evening." Baxter offered Mrs. Grenville a reprieve from being forced to play the pianoforte for their entertainment. Nonetheless, he couldn't help but appreciate that if she took to the keys, the males and females were evenly matched for dancing.

And blast his eyes, if he didn't want to take Miss Justina Farthington into his arms and whirl her about the room. Zounds, he'd like to do a lot more than that, and his immediate, compelling response to her puzzled him as much as it fascinated.

Glancing to the window, Baxter allowed the minutest upward tilt of his mouth.

Snow swirled furiously outside, blurring the view, and by the looks of the storm, his newest guests wouldn't be going anywhere anytime soon.

Why that delighted him, Baxter refused to examine.

3

Bathhurst Hotel and Spa
22 November 1810
Early Afternoon

Curled into an oversized chair covered in forest green and crimson brocade, Justina attempted to focus her attention on *Don Sebastian* by Anna Maria Porter, the book she'd selected from the surprisingly well-stocked library at Bathhurst Hotel and Spa. In truth, she was astonished to find the volume which had only been released last year.

However, the story failed to hold her attention as she'd hoped, and as her mind often had the past days, her thoughts mulishly migrated to Baxter Bathhurst.

The dratted man had her at sixes and sevens, and she wasn't the sort of empty-headed ninny to have her head turned by a captivating smile or a disarming glint in an attractive man's eyes.

No, indeed.

Not until now.

It was simply astonishing and so out of character for her as well.

A very unladylike snort escaped Justina.

Typically, she strove to abide by Society's strictures and did her utmost not to draw undesirable attention, much less say or do anything to cause a raised eyebrow, censorious look, or titillating whisper. Except, she *had* joined several other ladies in Hyde Park early one morning last summer, and they'd dared to ride astride, some even brazenly wearing breeches.

Scandalous.

Yes, and ever so wonderful.

A secret smile bent her mouth at the memory.

Mayhap that yearning to be more daring and bolder that she kept rigorously subdued meant to rebel at its confinement.

Heaven help her. She mustn't allow it.

Wasn't her illegitimacy disgrace enough?

Wasn't her contrived relationship with Aunt Emily sufficient to ruin them both should the truth ever be learned?

Hadn't her adopted aunt sacrificed and risked everything for Justina?

By all that was holy, she *would* control the wicked streak in her—a tendency Justina must've inherited from her mother.

Or perchance her father, as well, since she had absolutely no idea who *he* was. She'd seen a miniature of Richard Farthington, and Justina didn't recognize him. If he'd fathered her, he'd cut her mother from his life long before that fateful day a decade ago that had left Justina orphaned.

With renewed determination, Justina firmed her lips, pressing them into a hard line as her fingers curled into the book's pages.

She *would* resist her wayward tendencies.

I must.

In truth, neither she nor Aunt Emily had expected

they'd be delayed this long in Bath. Though the snow had finally stopped in the late afternoon two days ago, at least two-and-one-half feet of thick white covered the ground, rendering coach travel impossible until it melted.

Justina wasn't the least put out regarding their forced stay, and she was honest enough to admit that her enigmatic host was the cause.

To be precise, her befuddling reaction to Baxter Bathhurst was the reason.

In the days since her arrival, she'd reluctantly realized she'd looked for Baxter quite often—*oh, very well, constantly*—and as the guests and their host took all of their meals together, she'd seen him at least thrice daily. Then there were the after-supper interactions, the day he'd introduced her to his birds, and the four times he'd appeared in the parlor during tea.

It was silly, she well knew, but Justina wished the frequent encounters were because he sought her out.

Cabbage head.

Her heart gave that delicious fluttering movement

it did whenever her musings drifted in his direction.

God help her; she had it bad. Very bad, indeed.

How could it have happened so quickly?

Staring blankly at the open pages, she shook her head.

Aunt Emily would be horrified had she any notion. Which of course, Justina would make absolutely sure she never had the slightest inkling.

"You're a besotted idiot," Justina chastised herself beneath her breath, even though she was alone in the greenhouse's almost tropical setting. The other guests didn't favor the birds as much as she and, even confined in their cages as the exotic birds were, the Popkin sisters were quite terrified of the winged menagerie.

That suited Justina perfectly fine.

This bit of heaven was hers, and hers alone, to enjoy since the day Baxter had introduced her to the greenhouse and its avian guests. Today was the first day Princess and Duke hadn't followed her into her sanctuary.

Instead, Duke's paw now much recovered, they'd

gone for a walk with Baxter.

Who, Justina asked herself, walked in the freezing cold with snow up to their knees?

Baxter Bathhurst, that was who.

There was so much about him that she wanted to know and didn't dare ask.

Where did he hail from?

Did he have any sisters or brothers?

Were his parents alive? What were his favorite foods? What had motivated him to hire his unique collection of servants? And why rescue unusual birds?

Possibly it was boredom that had Justina so consumed with thoughts of her host. Even as she considered the possibility, Justina dismissed it for the fustian rot that it was.

Baxter—how utterly wicked of her to think of him this way—had permitted her to feed a parrot and a cockatoo a bite of apple that first morning. Now, she was allowed to feed all of the birds a treat or two anytime she wished.

Having never before been infatuated, Justina assumed the eagerness to see Baxter—to look upon him, into his warm, caramel brown eyes, and to hear his rumbling baritone—was infatuation. His tenor held an inflection, the merest melodious accent she couldn't quite place but which teased Justina's ears and made him all that much more mysterious and intriguing.

Tantalizing. Fascinating. Enthralling.

And so many more words ending in *ing*.

Although she'd been ten years of age when she'd arrived in England, and it had taken her two years to learn to speak the language fluently, she hadn't retained a German accent. At least not one that was detectable, and Aunt Emily had assured her it was so. Not that it mattered, for Justina's Austrian heritage was well-known, and she wasn't ashamed of it.

From the corner of her eye, a movement caught her attention. She glanced out the window, her book forgotten at what she beheld.

Baxter shoveled snow from the curved walkway.

He'd returned from his outing then.

From beneath her lashes, Justina observed him— for to stare outright would be most ill-mannered— quite enjoying the way his jacket pulled taut across his broad back and shoulders as he worked. He was inarguably handsome, his strong jaw, slightly hooked nose, and weather-touched features perhaps too rugged for le *beau monde's* standard of attraction compared to the pale-faced, mincing fops in London.

He turned to begin clearing another row, and a shock of sandy-brown hair fell over his forehead. The errant locks made him look younger, more boyish and carefree. Not that he was old, by any means.

She'd wager he hadn't reached his thirties yet, but there was an air about him as if he were burdened or perhaps troubled.

Little puffs of air floating from his much too alluring and well-formed mouth as he repeatedly inserted the broad, flat shovel into the snow and then heaved the load to the side gave testament to the frigid temperature outdoors.

Inside the conservatory, heated pipes kept the space quite comfortable. Should Justina require it, a knitted emerald-colored afghan lay draped across the arm of a nearby sofa. Two more throws were stacked upon a nearby table.

Naturally, neither were necessary during the warmer months when, she imagined, the space might feel as tropical as it looked with all of the shrubs, plants, and citrus trees.

The occasional squawk of a bird rent the tranquility every now and again, but Justina had become so accustomed to the birds' sounds, she scarcely noticed any longer. In point of fact, she rather liked the chirps and chatter, and a desire to explore the places where these birds had originated swept her.

Baxter tossed another shovel of heavy snow with the ease of one emptying a dustbin.

Wasn't he cold?

He swiped a forearm across his forehead.

Well, perhaps not, given the rigorousness of the activity. It somewhat surprised Justina that, as the owner of the hotel, he didn't think himself above physical labor. She had been introduced to gentlemen and peers that she was convinced didn't even prepare their own toothbrushes.

As if sensing her perusal, Baxter glanced up, and a slow, devilish grin tilted his firm mouth upward. He winked—*the wicked man actually winked!*—before returning to his task.

A tremor, much like the one that had skittered up Justina's spine when he'd taken her in his arms to dance the other night, caused her to shudder again.

She could still feel his iron-like arms embracing her, smell the masculine scent of his cologne—something woodsy-mossy with a hint of cloves and leather—and see the faintest dark stubble on his jaw. She closed her eyes, savoring the memory, the feel of his legs brushing hers as they waltzed, how they moved in such perfect timing, swaying and dipping—

No! Cease this instant!

Justina popped her eyelids open and clapped the book shut, setting it aside as she lowered her feet to the floor. After donning her slippers, she considered joining Aunt Emily in the spa but then, upon further consideration, decided against it.

She'd satisfied her curiosity about *taking the cure* the day after their arrival. Truth be told, the experience had left much to be desired. Guests were offered earthy tasting, cloudy water. They relaxed upon chaise lounges, sipping the less than appetizing beverage. If one wished, a bath in the mineral water could also be arranged.

Justina wrinkled her nose.

No, thank you very much.

It was said the waters were a cure for a myriad of ailments, including leprosy and infertility. But as Justina boasted a strong constitution and had seldom been sick with so much as a head cold her entire life, she'd eschewed the experience.

She had no interest in visiting the acclaimed Bath Pump Room at a later date either.

Aunt Emily *had* indulged in taking the waters and a bath but had declared a rather annoying film had stuck to her skin afterward, and she feared she smelled like rotten eggs. That was the salt in the chloride, Baxter had explained. The minerals were the cause of the murky tint to the waters as well.

How did a simple hotelier know such a specific detail?

Well, Baxter did own a spa, and it did seem reasonable he'd educate himself about the history of the hot spring, Justina supposed.

A gorgeous blue macaw named Romero cocked his head and lifted a foot, his version of a wave. He then billed the latch to his cage, more of a good-sized rectangular pen.

Ah, he wanted out.

Baxter had shown her which of the birds were permitted to fly about the greenhouse as long as the doors were firmly shut. Astonishingly, some of the birds returned to their cages when they needed to relieve themselves, for which Justina was most grateful.

Once she'd checked the outer door to assure it was shut tight, she made her way to the other, which opened into a small covered courtyard that led to the main house. Before she reached the doorway, however, Godfrey Howlette swaggered into the conservatory.

Had he been drinking this early in the day?

It wouldn't be the first time he'd imbibed before the midday meal. The man tottered about half-pished most of the time. What was more, he ogled her in a most disconcerting fashion as well. This, however, was the first occasion they'd been alone together, and at once, unease prickled her skin and took to wing in her belly.

It was also the first occasion he'd actually ventured into the greenhouse while she'd been a guest at Bathhurst Hotel and Spa.

Had Mr. Howlette sought her out, knowing she'd be alone?

"Ah, there you are, Miss Farthington."

His mouth pinching in distaste, Howlette cast a fleeting glance at the birds.

So his venturing here wasn't out of any admiration for the flora or fauna.

"I wondered where you'd hidden yourself away these past few days," he said.

Retreating to the center of the room to put more space between herself and Mr. Howlette, who had the disgusting habit of staring at her bosoms while running his tongue over his lower lip, Justina squared her shoulders.

"I assure you, I am not *hiding* away, Mr. Howlette." *Boorish buffoon.* "I am simply particular about whose company I keep."

Her dart hit home, and in an instant, his affable expression transformed into annoyance.

"I do hope you aren't referring to me," he remarked casually as he closed the door behind him with a distinct and rather portentous *snick*. "*I* am the nephew of an earl," he informed her with an air of great self-importance, his nose elevated in a haughty manner.

La de da.

A thread of unease traipsed across Justina's shoulders, and she speared a glance at the window where she'd seen Baxter shoveling snow earlier.

Drat and blast.

He was gone.

She'd hoped... Well, she didn't know precisely what she'd expected.

Yes, she did.

She'd hoped he'd notice what was occurring in the greenhouse and save her from this wretched man company.

"Mr. Howlette, unfortunately"—*fortunately for*

me—"you've caught me just as I was leaving." Romero's exercise would have to wait, poor bird. "My aunt is expecting me."

Howlette advanced toward her, his movements predatory and calculating, a smug smile quirking the edges of his too-full lips.

"Justina," he drawled with an alarming gleam in his gaze.

"May I call you Justina? It's such a lovely name."

A shudder of revulsion rippled through her.

"We are rather like a family here at Bathhurst, are we not? Dining together, seeing one another all day, *sleeping* under the same roof."

The way he said sleeping raised her hackles, and she'd wager her virtue that his lewd gaze sank to her bosoms before she counted to three.

One, two…

His lascivious focus slid to her breasts again.

"No, you may not. And no, we assuredly are *not*," Justina snapped.

She made to move past him, but the boor stepped in front of her. She stepped to the left, and once again, he blocked her way, that oily smile yet skewing his mouth.

"What childish game do you play?" Thoroughly miffed with his machinations, she planted her hands on her hips. "As I already said, my aunt is expecting me. I am tardy in meeting her as it is."

God forgive her for that little taradiddle.

Howlette's smile grew slyer still. "I know for a fact that your aunt is having a lie-down. She has the headache and retired to her chamber nearly half an hour ago."

And this unscrupulous rat took the opportunity to seek me out.

"Then all the more reason for me to go to her."

What was the rotter about?

Was she going to have to be rude?

Howlette stepped nearer, so near Justina could smell the spirits he'd been imbibing, as well as sweat and a whiff of garlic. Nonetheless, she resisted the urge to back away.

This churl would not intimidate her.

She couldn't, however, prevent her nostrils from

flaring or narrowing her eyes.

"From the moment I laid eyes upon you, Justina Farthington, I knew there was something special between us." He brazenly traced a finger along her jaw, his attention once more trained on her bodice. "I'm sure we can find a pleasurable way to relieve the godawful tedium of being housebound."

"You go beyond the mark, sir." She jerked her face away and beat a tactical retreat as she furtively sought a weapon of some sort. The fireplace was too far away to avail herself of the poker.

How much damage could an apple thrown at his head do?

Not enough.

He pursued her, advancing a menacing stride for everyone step she retreated.

"If you do not let me pass, I shall scream."

Grabbing her upper arms, he hauled her to him, wrenching a gasp from her. He smiled lecherously. "I *like* it when my women scream."

What the devil?

"I beg your pardon?"

He likes—

Thrusting a hand into her hair, Howlette jerked hard, and tears sprang to Justina's eyes even as she heard her hairpins pinging onto the stone floor.

Jerking her head from side to side to avoid his slobbering mouth upon her face, she feared she might be sick or perhaps faint.

No, you shall not!

This wasn't the time for feminine hysterics or weaknesses.

Her mind whirled, even as she struggled to escape his punishing grasp. If she could manage a few inches between them, she'd knee him in his man parts. "Let go of—"

Howlette mashed his wet lips onto Justina's, and she nearly gagged. Her struggles became more violent as panic swirled in her middle.

Would anyone come looking for her?

Aunt Emily was probably sound asleep by now.

If Justina managed to scream, could anyone hear her?

Like a man possessed by a demonic force,

Howlette tore frantically at the neckline of her gown.

Oh, God.

Was she about to be ravished?

Several birds cried out in alarm.

Justina tried to clamp her mouth shut, but when Howlette groped her, painfully squeezing and laughing maniacally against her lips, she gasped. In an instant, he shoved his tongue into her mouth.

She did gag then and renewed her exertions.

Howlette wouldn't have his way with her without a colossal battle, by heavens. She'd tear his hair out, bite, scratch, kick…

The conservatory's outer door crashed open, and a primitive, enraged animalistic cry echoed through the space.

The birds erupted into a deafening chorus of frightened calls and squawks.

Before Justina could comprehend what was happening, Howlette had been yanked from her and spun around.

Unsteady and her arms flailing, she stumbled backward, almost falling. Then in a blink, comprehension dawned.

Baxter.

Oh, thank God, Thank God.

Scalding tears leaked from her eyes as she hugged her arms around her waist, rocking slightly. Her lungs burned, and her tight throat throbbed from the effort to hold back her sobs.

He'd come.

He'd really, truly come.

She'd wished him here, and here he was.

His mouth curled into a feral snarl, Baxter swept a furious gaze over Justina, taking in her bruised lips and her hair tumbling haphazardly about her shoulders before his enraged gaze sank to her chest.

In horror, she realized Howlette had ripped the fabric of her gown, and it hung loose, exposing her breasts. Mortified, she snatched the torn remnants together, a hatred like she'd never known billowing through her in undulating waves.

If she were a man, she'd call the scapegrace out.

If you were a man, you'd not be in this situation.

"Come now, Bathhurst," Howlette wheedled,

prying at Baxter's fists clenching his coat lapels. "You're a hot-blooded man. You know how some women are." He gave a knowing wink. "The trollop wanted it. She's been teasing me since she arrived. Wiggling her bum and thrusting her—"

"Ye rotted, bloody scunner," Baxter roared, plowing his fist into Howlette's face, breaking his nose. Bone crunched, and blood spurted.

Scots. That's what the accent is.

Justina fought an absurd urge to burst into laughter at the ill-timed epiphany.

Howling, Howlette staggard and swayed.

"That was for touchin' her," Baxter growled savagely. "This one is for speakin' such filth about her."

The second blow drove Howlette to his knees. His eyes rolled back into his head, and he pitched, face-first, onto the floor.

Shoulders heaving and his breath coming in short heavy rasps, Baxter raised his kind brown eyes, now brimming with concern and compassion, to Justina's shocked gaze.

"Justina?"

And then, as if it were the most natural thing in the whole world, he held out his arms.

Without being aware she'd even moved, she flew into his embrace.

4

As Justina clung to Baxter, great tremors shaking her trim figure, he nuzzled her hair and spoke Gaelic in low, comforting tones. He ran his palms up and down her delicate spine and across her shoulders.

Baxter well knew he overstepped the bounds, taking it upon himself to soothe her, but he could no more prevent himself from doing so than he could from thrashing Howlette for taking liberties. From the moment he'd seen Justina in the drawing room, there'd been something about her that connected with him in an almost tangible way.

It made no sense, but who was he to question the mystery of it?

He drew her minutely closer, savoring the

sensation. Her form fit his so perfectly, curve to curve and angle to angle, that it rather stunned him. He could hold her this way forever.

"I thought he—" she managed in a choked, stricken voice, her body quaking. "If you hadn't come—"

She shook her head against his chest, and the faint odor of orange blossoms and lemon verbena wafted upward. She smelled like spring and sunshine and meadows.

"Hush now," he soothed. "You're safe, lass. He'll be gone within the hour, I promise you, sweet."

Baxter reined his brogue under control once more, but the vestiges of his earlier wrath still thrummed hotly through his veins and pounded in his temples. He'd wanted to kill that sniveling blackguard for laying a finger on Justina. Even now, as Howlette lay semi-conscious, Baxter barely suppressed the impulse to kick him in the ribs.

He wasn't confident Justina was able to return to the main hotel under her own strength, and he wasn't leaving Howlette without giving the filthy bounder a tongue lashing. He flexed his fingers, still wanting to pummel the blackguard to ten Sundays from now.

Baxter glanced around for something to cover her torn gown and restore her modesty and spied one of the throws he'd commissioned Widow Honeybun to make for the hotel.

"Can you stand on your own, Justina?" he asked, mindful to keep his fulminating fury from seeping into his voice.

Justina nodded, and head tucked to her chin and clutching her ruined bodice, she stepped from his embrace.

At once, he felt the oddest sense of bereftness.

How much worse would it be when she left Bathhurst Hotel and Spa?

Before she left, he intended to ask if he could call upon her. The draw to her was that strong, that compelling, that…irresistible.

She swayed slightly, and Baxter clasped her shoulders, steadying her.

"I'm going to collect the throw just there, so you can cover yourself, Justina."

Eyes downcast, her lashes a dark fan against her waxen cheeks, she nodded again but remained silent.

If anyone should come upon them, she'd be utterly ruined. No one must know of this, and as the Duke of San Sebastian, he meant to put the fear of God in Howlette. He'd annihilate the bugger if he breathed a single syllable about what had transpired between him and Justina in the conservatory. Blackguards like him liked to brag about their prowess and conquests.

In a trice, Baxter had retrieved the soft, knitted afghan and fashioned it into a makeshift shawl. He draped it across Justina's creamy shoulders, and she accepted the ends and gathered them together in front, effectively hiding her gown's dishevelment. Except for her hair, to anyone happening upon her, it appeared she'd become chilled and wrapped herself in the fine wool to stay warm.

"Justina, please sit for a moment while I deal with him."

Baxter guided her to the chair the farthest from Howlette.

A gardenia, two large, ornate birdcages, as well as

potted orange and lemon trees brought inside for the winter partially obstructed the view. That worked to his benefit quite nicely.

After seeing her comfortably seated, Baxter squatted before her.

"Justina, please stay here. I'll return shortly and scout a path to your chamber so that no one sees you. There are back corridors we can use to assure your privacy."

"Thank you, Baxter."

Her light green eyes, fringed by damp sooty lashes, held a hint of her usual spirit.

Unable to help himself, he touched her cheek with his fingertips, encountering skin as soft and smooth as a rose petal. "You're very welcome."

What did one say when a woman thanked one for saving her from being violated?

Certainly not, "My pleasure," or "Anytime, or "I hope to do so again."

Her cheeks turned a becoming pink, and she fixed her gaze on her lap.

"I'll be but a few minutes," he assured her.

In a half dozen lengthy strides, he returned to Howlette, now sitting up, his shoulders slumped while he held a bloodied handkerchief to his nose.

He glared at Baxter, pure hatred spewing from his bloodshot eyes, one already starting to blacken nicely. Wincing, the spoiled assling muttered, "So help me, you'll pay for this Bathhurst. *I'm* practically aristocracy," he declared with pompous pride. "You'll soon regret laying hands on your betters. *My* uncle is an earl. An *earl*, I tell you. I vow you'll regret the day you attacked me, *Scotsman*."

The last word he spat as if his mouth was full of offal.

"An *earl?*" Baxter arched a brow as he towered over Howlette. "Ye dinna say."

"Indeed," Howlette snuffled into the soiled cloth while trying to attempt an air of arrogance and failing miserably.

"The Earl of Torrens." He narrowed his eyes to insolent slits. "He'll see you destroyed, Bathhurst. No one will visit your rustic hotel when he's finished with you. I'll have you charged with assault causing bodily harm. You'll soon find yourself rotting away in prison."

Pretentious windbag.

Baxter chuckled as he examined a torn fingernail.

Had that happened while shoveling snow or when he'd punched this poltroon?

Lowering himself to his haunches, he was gratified to see Howlette's eyes widen in renewed fright as he nervously scampered backward like a wounded crab.

Romero laughed and, pointing a claw at the coward, screeched in a sing-song voice, "Idi-ot. Idi-ot."

The parrot had belonged to a traveling entertainer for twenty years. When the man died, no one knew what to do with the obstinate bird who spoke only when he deuced well felt like it.

"Well then, do tell Torrens that the *Duke* of San Sebastian sends his greetings," Baxter said, making certain to keep his voice low enough that Justina wouldn't overhear. He didn't want word of his title to become common knowledge around here, just yet.

It was rather disconcerting and not just a little inconvenient how behavior toward him changed when people knew he was titled, and more so that he was a reluctant duke. He'd much prefer to be treated like any other ordinary man and judged on his character and actions rather than the lofty title bestowed upon him.

Howlette's jaw unhinged, sagging to his chin in a most undignified manner.

"And do make sure you mention *you* were intent on defiling an innocent young woman," Baxter drawled, driving home his point.

"D…D…Duke of San Sebastian?" Howlette croaked, his voice a quavering, sliver of a sound. "You?" he squeaked. "You're a…*duke*?"

The wry smile Baxter curved his mouth into didn't begin to express his satisfaction at the stupefaction of the maggot before him.

"Indeed, I am." Baxter leaned forward.

"And, you sodding scum, a duke *always* outranks an earl. Therefore, I'll say this very clearly so that there are absolutely no misunderstandings between us.

You will depart Bathhurst Hotel and Spa within a quarter-hour. You will not speak of what occurred here to anyone. *Ever*. And you will, from this point forward, do your utmost to never encounter Miss Farthington or me again."

Baxter rose to his full height, and though not overly tall at eleven inches over five feet, he was well-muscled, unlike the quaking fop before him.

He speared Howlette with a murderous glare.

"If you *ever* so much as think of Miss Farthington, much less speak her name…I. Shall. Destroy. *You.* You'll have to leave England, for I'll use every resource available to me as a duke to see you ostracized. Even your dear uncle won't acknowledge you by the time I'm done with destroying your character."

Baxter glanced toward Justina, still huddled on the chair, her face averted. Renewed rage sluiced through him as he turned his attention back to Howlette. "Understood?"

The little remaining color in Howlette's pasty face

drained away, and he gave a single stiff nod.

Baxter watched him struggle to his feet and leave the greenhouse, idly wondering what cock and bull excuse he'd give for his shabby appearance should anyone happen upon him.

Cupping his nape, he turned toward Justina.

She'd risen and, though still slightly wan, looked to have composed herself as well as had managed to restore her hair to some semblance of order.

"You're Scots?"

Of all the things she could've said, that wasn't what he'd expected.

"Aye."

Head tilted, she asked, "How did you come to own a hotel in Bath?"

He scratched his brow, giving her a sideways glance. "It's a long story. Much too long to tell right now."

"I see." She gave a little nod and turned toward the door Howlette had disappeared through.

Baxter touched her elbow.

"I'll tell you someday if you'd truly like to know, Justina, but for now, I think it imperative you go to your chamber and change your gown. I assure you, Howlette will keep his mouth shut."

She gave another nod before suddenly turning back to him.

"Baxter…?"

Justina licked her lower lip, and he stifled a groan.

What a colossal arse he was, finding such a simple action alluring when she'd undergone the shock of her life.

"Yes, Justina?"

She hurried back to him, stood up on her toes, and brushed butterfly wing soft lips across his cheek.

Baxter remained stone still, afraid to so much as blink lest his control snap.

He desired her.

Lord above, how he wanted her.

Wanted to know everything about this intriguing woman who managed to upend his world in such a short time. What was more, he wanted to protect her, and while he'd always treated women with respect, never had there been this gripping desire to safeguard one.

"Thank you. I'll never forget what you've done for me," Justina murmured, a delightful flush skating dual paths up her cheeks. Her attention slid to his mouth, and she bit her lower lip.

"Justina? I..."

Och, hell's bells.

Then she was in his arms, where she ought to remain for the rest of their lives, and Baxter was brushing the unbearable sweetness of her lips with his.

She sighed and relaxed against him, her fragrance wafting around them, intoxicating and dizzying.

Eyes closed, he savored every second, trying to memorize the moment, the smells, the taste, the feelings.

Her lips moved beneath his, and his soul rejoiced.

Justina clung to him, her kisses unpracticed but fervent.

Bliss. Pure bliss.

"Kiss me. Kiss me." A parrot's grating voice interrupted the magical moment. "Ki-iss."

The parrot started making loud smooching noises.

Bloody, annoying bird.

Pulling away, Justina settled back onto the balls of her feet. Her soft green eyes wide in wonderment, she touched her fingertips to her crimson lips. Then, without a word, she turned on her heels and fled.

5

Bathhurst Hotel and Spa

That evening

*M*y *God.* Justina had almost been violated. Ruined. Compromised.

She pressed trembling hands to her fluttering tummy, renewed fear washing over her. She could scarcely conceive what had occurred. It was like something from a Gothic novel. Young women of good repute were not set upon by a gentleman in a hotel conservatory.

What was this world coming to when such things occurred?

When gentlemen preyed upon women?

When she'd witnessed Baxter charging into the greenhouse, his expression fierce and intent, a vengeful Highland warrior, her heart had leaped in relief and also in a jot of apprehension.

Never had she observed such primal or violent behavior.

Nonetheless, Howlette had deserved the pummeling he'd received, and she couldn't summon a speck of sympathy or compassion for the blackguard. God rot his soul. May he burn in the ninth circle of hell for eternity.

She troubled her lower lip as the thought that had plagued her since she'd returned to her chamber hours ago reared its ugly, pointed head again.

Would Howlette keep his word?

Would he truly never speak of the incident?

How would he explain his injuries, then?

Well, a tale contrived about drunkards attacking him at a tavern would suffice, she supposed. A man of Howlette's ilk would have no trouble manufacturing believable twaddle.

Baxter had assured her Howlette wouldn't breathe

a word, but how could he be positive?

Inhaling a cleansing breath, Justina lifted a shoulder in an attempt to shake off her doleful ruminations. She released the air slowly through her nostrils, the deliberate act steadying her jangled nerves.

Quite simply, it was a matter of Godfrey Howlette's word against hers.

He could prove nothing. *Nothing.*

Yes, but since when did gossipmongers care about the truth?

Just the mere suggestion of impropriety was enough to send the chinwags' tongues into a wagging frenzy. And there were always ears too ready to listen to claptrap and hogwash.

As Justina glanced in the cheval mirror and tucked a stray strand of hair into place with a pin, she canted her head. She didn't look different in her mint green and rose petal pink gown, a green ribbon threaded through her dark curls.

Nevertheless, she was irreversibly changed.

Within a span of a few minutes, she'd experienced a taste of the worst and best life had to offer. Baxter's kiss

Marvelous.

Sensational.

Wondrous.

A bevy of words, yet none entirely accurate.

Baxter had kindled a conflagration in her, and every pore, every nerve, every part of her being wanted more. More. Lord, yes, *more.*

Closing her eyes against the reflection gazing back at her, equal parts cynical and expectant, Justina groaned.

She'd kissed Baxter.

Brazen as any dockside strumpet, she'd risen on her toes and pressed her lips against his firm, faintly rough cheek. A man she'd known but a week.

What could she have been thinking?

She'd wanted to show him her appreciation, but more than that, she'd wished to convey he meant something to her, and she mightn't ever have the opportunity to be alone with him again. Certainly, it was foolish and impulsive and unequivocally irrational.

But then *he'd* kissed her... Oh, that glorious, marvelous kiss.

A flush heated her from her waist to her hairline, and tingles sparked all over her body.

Good Lord.

She hadn't known what to expect for her first kiss, though naturally, she'd dreamed about it. Her daydreams didn't come close to the glorious reality.

Nor could she have imagined the bone-melting warmth or the unhinging of her knees or the small inferno he'd ignited in her middle and which still smoldered—secretly and naughtily—deep within her. And which flamed to life whenever she thought about Baxter.

Which, in all honesty, was nearly every second of every minute since she'd fled the greenhouse. Being held in his iron-like arms, cradled against the granite wall of his chest, inhaling his unique scent, and all the while, his mouth had explored hers tumbled around in her mind. No one had ever mentioned anything about tongues tangling erotically during kissing.

What else had she been kept oblivious of?

Thank all the divine powers, she hadn't come upon anyone as she'd rushed to her room using the servants' passageways. Justina would've been hard put to explain not only her disheveled state but her swollen lips and high color.

Aunt Emily mustn't ever know of either the kiss or that Justina had been set upon by Howlette. The poor dear might very well retire them both to the country. Although Justina wasn't entirely comfortable in crowds, neither did she wish to be relegated to the far corner of England to rusticate until her face wrinkled and her hair grayed.

In truth, the kiss she'd shared with Baxter had rattled her comportment every bit as much as Howlette's assault. The latter she never wished to experience again, but the former...

She opened her eyes once more, seeking the bedside clock.

In fifteen minutes, she'd join the guests in the drawing room for their usual pre-dinner libation.

How could she face Baxter?

With grace and aplomb, she commanded herself.

In the manner Aunt Emily had taught her. A lady always presents herself with decorum and composure no matter what she may be thinking or feeling.

As Justina placed her hand on the door latch, another unwelcome thought intruded, and she instinctively put a hand to her hair.

My hairpins.

Several had dislodged during Howlette's rough treatment. If someone came upon the hairpins scattered on the conservatory floor, they were sure to raise speculation.

True, but no one would know the pins belonged to her, and there weren't so very many pins—perhaps six or so.

Ten minutes later, Justina stood with a glass of untouched sherry in her hand, half-listening to Mildred Popkin prattle on about whether taking the waters had improved her arthritis and the tale of her godlike Prussian prince she'd met during her first season.

Sixty years ago.

Baxter and Aunt Emily had yet to make an appearance, and Justina briefly considered going in search of her aunt. She swiftly dismissed the notion. If Aunt Emily were indisposed with one of her megrims, she'd have let Justina know.

But where was Baxter?

Was he avoiding her after their kiss?

He'd never been tardy to the pre-dinner gathering before. A *beau monde* peer would be hard-pressed to outshine Baxter as a host. His attention to detail and to his guests' comfort was exceptional.

"Everyone deserves to be treated like royalty, if only for a short time," he'd declared to his guests that first night.

"Most peculiar, don't you think so, Miss Farthington?" Mildred said, her tone conspiratorial.

Hearing her name snapped Justina back to the present.

The Popkin sisters peered at her, both with expectant expressions on their wrinkled faces as they blinked their faded brown eyes at her in unison behind their spectacles.

"I beg your pardon?" Justina offered a bright smile as an apology for allowing her mind to wander.

"Mr. Howlette," Marian Popkin chimed in.

Howlette?

Panicked filled Justina.

Oh, God.

What did they know?

She only managed a bland look as her mind scrambled, imagining one horrific scenario after another.

"His rather abrupt departure," Mildred provided helpfully.

"Um, yes," Justina said. "Perchance, Mr. Howlette feared another snowstorm would make the roads impassable once more."

For she'd learned from the chatty maid, Ginny, who'd prepared her bath, that the main roads were now fit for travel. This meant, in all likelihood, Justina and Aunt Emily would depart on the morrow.

Her stomach sank to her toes, and the oddest hollow sensation plagued her middle.

It was too soon.

Justina wasn't ready to leave. There was this thing between her and Baxter to explore. If she left, she'd never know what it was or what it might become.

But how on earth could she persuade Aunt Emily to stay on for a few days?

Ginny entered the drawing room and made straight for Justina. She bobbed a shallow curtsy, one hazel eye peering at Justina and the other pointing inward toward the girl's nose.

"Miss Farthington, your aunt bid me tell you she's indisposed this evening, after all."

Concerned, Justina put her glass aside. "I shall go to her at once."

Heavens above.

What kind of a horrid person was she?

She'd not even inquired after Aunt Emily's headache.

"No, Miss." Shaking her head, the maid gave a lopsided smile. "She said you'd say that. You're to enjoy your evening, as she plans to depart tomorrow, the weather and her health permitting."

It was settled then.

Justina and her aunt were to leave. And Justina wanted to wail like an infant at the unfairness of it.

"Very well. Thank you, Ginny."

With another bob, the maid departed.

"So, you're leaving tomorrow, *too*?" His grizzly brows contorting, Major Spaulding glanced around the room. "I do believe we all intend to depart within the next day or two."

"Indeed," Paul Harmon provided with an adoring glance at his blushing bride. "We're anxious to set up house and start a family."

His wife's cheeks grew hopelessly redder.

The tiniest pinch of envy poked Justina at the palpable love the Harmons shared. Beyond a dance or a partner for piquet, no man had shown any marked interest in her. She'd often wondered, quite uncharitably given all that her adopted aunt had done for her, if Emily had warned them away somehow.

Or perhaps it was that she was Austrian. She was dowerless, and that eliminated a great many beaus and suitors. In particular, those in need of a fortune for one reason or another.

"Ah, there's our host now," boomed the major, puffing out his chest as was his wont.

Justina couldn't prevent her attention from seeking Baxter out.

Tonight, he wore a stylish superfine woolen coat in the deepest blue. His black trousers enhanced his long legs, and not even Beau Brummel himself could find fault with the intricate folds of his cravat.

His warm honey gaze met hers from across the room, and a powerful current traveled between them until Marian Popkin tapped his arm, demanding his attention. "This has been a delightful respite, Mr. Bathhurst. You may rest assured. My sister and I shall encourage our friends to visit and take the cure. And we will be back in July."

"Thank you, Miss Popkin," he demurred, glancing over her silvery head to search out Justina.

She couldn't prevent the pleased smile teasing the edges of her mouth.

~*~

Dinner passed in a haze as Justina attempted polite conversation with the major on her left and Mildred on her right. She scarcely tasted the meal since all of her concentration was focused on not staring at Baxter.

She thought perhaps there'd been white soup and fowl of some sort.

Duck? Partridge? Chicken? *Quail*?

There *had* been mashed peas. That Justina clearly remembered, for she detested peas. Particularly those squished into green goo.

And dessert had been…?

Something soft and sweet. Pudding perhaps.

Over and over and over, Justina's attention had shied toward Baxter. And, by heavens, several times, she'd found his hooded gaze trained upon her. It thrilled her in a most enticing way.

Never had a man affected her so. Mayhap the shock of being attacked had impacted her more than she'd realized, causing her current befuddlement.

At long last, dinner ended.

Deciding wisdom was the best course of action, she excused herself from the usual after-dinner activities before she made a complete cake of herself. A small frown pulled Baxter's brows together, and his mouth curved downward the merest bit at her announcement.

Was he disappointed?

Justina fought the giddiness such a notion caused.

They'd shared a kiss. *One kiss*. A kiss she'd instigated.

She was a fool to make more of it than that.

She paused outside Aunt Emily's chamber and knocked softly upon the door.

"Aunt Emily?" No answer was forthcoming. Justina tried the handle. Finding it locked securely, she whispered, "Good night, Aunt Emily. Sleep well."

Tomorrow they'd leave this place, perhaps never to return, and Justina couldn't help but feel like her life had been irreversibly changed these past few days. Like a river burbling downhill and splitting in two directions. She'd been on one course, and now she was on another, only she had no idea what the outcome would be or where she'd end up.

Deep in thought, she continued on to her chamber.

After removing her gown and brushing her hair, Justina wrapped another of the exquisitely knitted throws about her shoulders and settled into a chair. Staring at the fire, she replayed her kiss with Baxter over and over in her head until sleep claimed her.

Awakening sometime later, Justina stretched and yawned.

A glance at the bedside clock revealed the time to be half-past eleven. After slipping her chemise off and donning her night rail, she blew out all but one candle.

Was Baxter abed?

Was he thinking about their kiss too?

Unable to sleep after her nap, Justina wandered to the window and pushed aside the draperies. Today's sun had melted much of the snow, but a goodly amount still covered the ground, especially in the shaded areas.

This was the rear of the hotel. It faced what she guessed might be a charming garden in the summer. Her focus fell upon a lone figure standing with his hands clasped behind his back and his head turned upward, staring at the star-strewn sky.

Baxter.

What was it about that man that called to her?

As if sensing her perusal, he slowly turned and

stared up at her window. She didn't move away or pretend maidenly shyness. He'd caught her staring at him again, yet somehow, she thought that rather pleased him.

A small cloud drifted over the moon, dousing the silvery light, and she squinted into the darkness.

He was gone.

She sighed and let the draperies slide shut once more.

Tomorrow they would leave.

Would it be too forward or fast to ask him if they might correspond?

She'd just pulled the bedcoverings back when a soft scratching sounded at her door, so faint that she thought she'd misheard.

It came again.

Had Aunt Emily's condition worsened?

On bare feet, she ventured near but, instead of throwing the door open, acquiesced to caution. Being attacked did that to a person.

"Who is it?"

"Baxter. I know it's late, but what I have to say

cannot wait until tomorrow. Can I come in for a minute, please?"

Firmly shoving prudence and good sense aside, Justina turned the lock, then pressed the handle and opened the door just enough for him to slip inside.

"Make haste," she whispered, trying not to notice he wore only his boots, trousers, and a fine lawn shirt open at the neck, the sleeves rolled to his elbows.

Baxter stepped near and drew a tendril of her hair over her shoulder.

"I have to leave before dawn, Justina. There's an issue at one of my businesses." *He has other businesses*? "I received word directly before we dined tonight."

Hence his tardiness.

"I would like permission to call on ye when I return. I ken it's sudden, and we dinna ken each other."

There was that melodious burr again.

Justina couldn't contain her smile.

"Isn't that what calling on me is for? So that we can come to know each other better?"

"Aye, lass. It is."

He wrapped those indecently muscled arms around her, edging her nearer and nearer until a scant couple of inches separated them.

"Then I have yer permission?"

Justina smiled up at him.

"You do, although Aunt Emily might not consent."

"Give me yer direction. Yer aunt can hardly boot me onto the street when I sound the knocker."

He didn't know Aunt Emily.

"I'll leave it with Mr. Bixby," Justina said, astonished at the throaty quality of her voice.

"I canna just let ye go."

Having slipped into his brogue, Baxter pressed his mouth to the crown of her head.

"I dinna ken what this is between us, but I've never felt anythin' like it, Justina."

"Me either," she whispered, trying and failing to ignore the springy hair visible where his shirt gaped open. Tilting her head upward, she met his blazing gaze and recognized her own need in his eyes.

"Kiss me, Baxter."

6

Baxter was only too happy to oblige.

In her diaphanous nightgown, the filmy fabric barely concealing Justina's womanly charms, she was Aphrodite, Freya, and Venus all wrapped into one tantalizing, fascinating, remarkable woman.

And by thunder, he wanted her.

God above, how he wanted her.

But he craved more than her lush body. There was a scintillating connection between him and Justina that went beyond physical attraction, and Baxter was convinced she felt it too. Even if she didn't understand precisely what it was.

Justina Farthington was not a woman of loose virtue or lax moral character. He'd seen her struggling against Howlette for all she was worth to preserve her virtue. And yet here she was, in Baxter's embrace, eagerly returning his kisses, her enthusiasm making up for her inexperience.

There wasn't a doubt in his mind that she hadn't a lot of practice kissing, and that knowledge inflamed him further. With a low, possessive sound deep in his throat, he tightened his arms, urging Justina nearer still.

Her little sighs and moans told him she was as overcome with passion as he.

This woman was his.

His!

Baxter felt it in the very marrow of his bones.

His swept his tongue against hers as he trailed a hand over the plump perfection of one buttock. She arched into him, and he groaned, angling Justina so he could trail hot kisses over her ivory neck and to the hollow at the juncture of her throat that had driven him crazy for days.

Inhaling, he tried to memorize her scent, to draw it inside him until it seared his very spirit. Oh, he'd bedded equally beautiful, voluptuous women before, but none had touched his soul, marking him as hers, as surely as if she'd branded him with her initials.

With a half-moan, half-groan, he gradually eased away from her, all the while playing his fingers lightly over her curves. He couldn't stop touching her, and it both thrilled and scared the devil out of him. No woman had ever affected him thus.

His carnal encounters had always been with willing, experienced females who craved a physical release. But this woman with her alabaster skin, pale green eyes, silky almond brown hair ribboned with golden and ashen streaks, and the two plump, kissable pillows of her mouth...

Breathing raggedly, Baxter grudgingly lifted his lips from hers and gave her *one, two, three* tender, quick kisses.

Did she have to taste so irresistibly sweet?

He was like a drunkard who couldn't drink enough ale or rum, always needing—craving—more. More. *More.*

"Baxter?" she said shakily, her voice sultry and

thick with desire. "My bed...?"

By thunder, she was offering herself to him.

A prized, unexpected gift he must refuse.

Och, I must.

It might very well kill him.

He gritted his teeth and prayed to God, all the saints, and even a few other deities to give him the strength to do what he had to. Deny her tempting offer. When he took Justina Farthington to bed, it would be as his wife, and when he could take as much time as he wanted to introduce her to the pleasures of the flesh.

That brought a satisfied grin to his mouth.

He didn't give a bloody curse that they'd only known each other mere days.

This was more than lust or desire.

It was a connection of spirits—one soul recognizing its mate against all odds.

"I canna, lass."

Baxter couldn't say all of the other things, wildly stupid and impetuous things on the tip of his tongue. *Yet.*

Disappointment pooled in her gorgeous green

eyes, still slightly glazed with passion. She bit her lower lip—red and plump and moist—and after a moment, averted her gaze while giving a stiff nod. "I…I understand."

No, she didn't. Not in the least.

He almost laughed aloud but feared he'd further humiliate her.

He'd be bound, Justina erroneously believed he didn't want her.

God help him; nothing was farther from the truth. But if Baxter didn't stop now, he wouldn't be able to, and he did have to leave before dawn tomorrow. He'd not love Justina, make her his, and leave her for weeks, wondering if he was sincere in his protestations. Fretting she'd given her virtue to a charlatan. Worried she might be with child.

Even in this short time, she meant too much to him to do that to her.

"I shall call upon you, Justina, when I return from Lancashire. My intentions toward you are honorable. I vow it."

He knew next to nothing about the woman gazing

at him so intently and slightly vulnerable as well. Aye, she was gently-bred and as refined as any lady he'd encountered in a *haut ton* ballroom. Her comportment was without flaw, and she was witty and kind and intelligent.

But he didn't know anything about her family, her past, or even what activities she enjoyed other than reading and feeding his birds.

I can discover all of that later.

What mattered was that he not lose this opportunity to make his interest clearly known, for whatever this was between them was rare and precious and should never, ever be disregarded. The caution and reason he was renowned for seemed to have flown to the farthest corners of the earth. And to his consternation and astonishment, he didn't give ten farthings.

The Baxter Bathhurst, Duke of San Sebastian, of a week ago would've had apoplexy at such a ludicrous notion.

With his forefinger, he lifted Justina's chin inch by inch until her eyes, those mesmerizing pools of green, met his. Dark blue-green rimmed her irises, and the palest yellow-green circled her pupils.

A trace of indecision crinkled the corners of her eyes the merest bit.

"Believe me, please."

Egads! He practically begged her. *He*, the Duke of San Sebastian, who'd never begged for anything.

Her eyes wide and her mouth slightly parted, Justina searched his face. Her expression cleared, her eyebrows relaxing, and serenity settled upon her delicate features.

"I do believe you, Baxter."

And she did.

He could see the trust in her guileless countenance, and that faith in him humbled Baxter.

"Let's see you to bed, then," he said. "I'm not sure how long I'll be away, but I cannot imagine it will be more than a week. Plus, travel time, of course."

A persistent grin tipped his mouth.

She nodded, and he couldn't help but notice her elegant neck again.

How could the sloping column of her neck be so

arousing?

Because it beckoned a man to look lower, to the round perfection of her shoulders and the seductive swell of breasts beneath the wholly inadequate fabric of her nightgown.

"That will give me time to tell Aunt Emily and for her to become accustomed to the idea."

A winsome smile teased the corners of her mouth.

He cocked his head. "Do you think she'll be opposed to me courting you?"

Honestly, Baxter hadn't considered that.

They dinna ken ye're a duke.

And he wanted to keep it that way for a while longer. Naturally, Justina would have to know eventually, but not yet. Baxter had to be convinced she wished to be with him because of who *he* was and for no other reason.

To Justina and Emily Grenville, he was merely a hotel proprietor. Not a disrespectable vocation by any means, but to those who aspired for loftier positions, anyone who worked for a living was inferior—smelled of the shop.

Truth be told, Mrs. Grenville wasn't even aware of his Scottish heritage. That, in and of itself, caused many of the *ton* to lift their haughty noses when he encountered them. As if he trod past with fresh horse manure clinging to his boots.

And yet, Justina had been fascinated by the knowledge that he was Scottish.

After guiding her to her bed and seeing her tucked beneath the plush coverlet, he sat beside her. He took her delicate hand in his.

"I know this is happening fast, Justina, but I shan't rush you. I'll call upon you in Bristol, and we'll see where this attraction between us goes. If you are agreeable, that is."

She must be.

Justina's mouth went slack before joy ignited in her eyes, radiating outward and lighting her face. She squeezed his hand. "It *is* fast. But I, for one, believe in love at first sight or short acquaintance. I know it's not common, but I am convinced it is real, nonetheless."

Love?

Who said anything about love?

She must've sensed Baxter's hesitancy, for in all honesty, he couldn't say he loved her. Not yet, in any event. She withdrew her hand, acute embarrassment evident in her strained features, the color tinging her cheeks, and her refusal to meet his gaze.

"I've spoken out of turn. Forgive me." She scooted farther beneath the bedcoverings, pulling them to beneath her chin. A fabric shield to ward off her discomfit.

"I'm very tired, Baxter, and need my rest. We're leaving tomorrow as well."

Confound it.

She'd retreated into herself, donning a mask of neutrality and politesse.

"Justina, I meant no offense."

"None was taken," she said softly.

Little liar.

Unable to help himself, Baxter brushed his hand across her smooth forehead and then fingered a lock of silky hair. The color was unusual, shifting and changing, depending on the light. In the muted glow of the candle, her hair shone like warm honey.

"Dinna forget to leave yer address with Bixby. I'd no' relish havin' to knock upon every door in Bristol to find ye."

She giggled, and the tension of a moment before dissipated. "You wouldn't. Not really."

"Ye dinna ken me, Justina. I would. When I put my mind to somethin', I'm no' easily dissuaded."

The tiniest furrow crinkled her brow as if she wasn't positive what to make of his declaration.

For a gem such as she, Baxter would bang upon every door in England *and* Scotland.

Baxter kissed her again, a tender sweep of his lips across hers.

It was as much a vow, a promise he'd seek her out after he'd attended to his duties, as much as a token of affection. Too many people depended on him for their well-being for him to ignore the problem. His overseer wouldn't have contacted Baxter if the situation hadn't been urgent.

Yet this reluctance to leave Justina Farthington, a woman he'd known but a week, made him wish, for once, he could cast his responsibilities aside. But even as the thought crossed his mind, he knew he would not. It wasn't his nature, and so he quirked his mouth into a tender smile.

"Good night, *leannan*."

"*Leannan*?" She tried the unfamiliar word. "That's Scots? What does it mean?"

"I'll tell you the next time I see you."

After another lingering taste of her delectable lips, he blew out the candle and left her chamber. Baxter couldn't check his broad smile as he sought his own room.

He hadn't seriously considered marrying so soon.

In truth, he'd spent a great deal of time avoiding the Marriage Mart. How fortunate could a man be that the perfect woman literally showed up on his doorstep? And most conveniently, was stranded there during a snowstorm?

If Baxter believed in Divine Providence—which, of course, he didn't—he just might be persuaded he'd somehow earned God's favor.

A wry chuckle escaped him at his fanciful musings.

What was it his mother used to say?

Och, aye. The Lord helps those who help themselves.

An hour later, as Baxter lay in his oversized bed, his hands clasped beneath his head, he stared up at the dark green canopy. The fire's capering flames cast irregular, elongated shadows onto the half-open bed curtains.

When should he tell Justina he held a title?

Very little chance existed that she'd learn that truth on her own. Therefore, he'd take his time and woo her. Not *too* much time, however.

He exhaled a frustrated breath.

Why had he given his word he'd attend the Sutcliffes' Christmastide house party?

Because Pennington, Bainbridge, and Westfall were pains in the arse who wouldn't take no for an answer. They believed Baxter worked too much and that he needed to take a holiday.

What sane man, in God's name, would choose to holiday in Essex in December?

Blast and bother.

Between the machinery issues at the textile factory and the holiday festivities, he'd have little time to court Justina.

Unless he could convince the Sutcliffes to invite her too?

No, he mightn't' know her well, but she didn't strike him as the type who was entirely at ease in crowds. Besides, she might be uncomfortable around so many peers.

What in blazes was he to do?

Bristol, England
15 December 1810

Brushing a hand across her forehead, Justina sighed for the umpteenth time. Eyebrows furrowed and her bottom lip clamped between her teeth, she considered the gowns laying upon her bed's light blue coverlet, trying to decide which she'd take to the Sutcliffes' house party.

None were new, but both she and Aunt Emily were gifted with a needle and thread, and gowns from two Seasons ago had been reworked quite satisfactorily. A scrap of lace here, a ribbon or braid there, or a new ruffle, and the garments were hardly recognizable. That was one practical means implemented to stretch coin.

Well, that was stretching the truth, but the frocks were near enough in style to the current fashion to pass the *haut ton's* inspection at first glance. And since Justina rarely drew a second glance, except from her friends, she wasn't concerned about her revamped wardrobe. That business of requiring new garments from the skin out each Season was positively wasteful.

Head tilted, she considered two additional morning gowns.

The mint green or the rose?

Both perhaps?

Justina wasn't above wearing a gown more than once at a house party. After all, budget and wardrobe restraints already required her to do so with other attire.

She slanted a glance at the nearly full trunk. It already contained three morning gowns, a riding habit, two walking ensembles, six afternoon gowns, and another half dozen evening gowns. Justina had also managed to fit a ballgown, a fichu, her unmentionables, a nightgown and robe, two each of spencers, pelisses, and shawls, and, lastly, a heavy cloak in case it snowed again.

Then there were gloves, shoes, stockings, her sewing kit, and various other necessary fallalls and fripperies. She almost envied servants their simple uniforms. *Almost.*

She'd wear her redingote and one of the three bonnets she intended to take with her in the coach.

Puffing out an unladylike sigh that ballooned her cheeks in a childish manner, Justina shook her head. Really. This would be so much easier, not to mention less costly, if women weren't required to change their gowns multiple times a day.

As neither she nor Aunt Emily employed a lady's maid, they acted as one another's abigail, as well as packed and unpacked their own trunks. Theadosia, Duchess of Sutcliffe, would assign them a maid to share for the duration of the house party, but it wasn't the least necessary.

For months, Justina had anticipated the Christmastide gathering, but now a shadow marred her earlier joy.

Baxter hadn't come knocking on her door.

He hadn't written either—not a single letter in over three weeks.

That isn't so very long, she tried to console herself.

True, but if Baxter had written promptly upon returning to Bath—

But—*drat the man*—he hadn't.

Deciding there was room for both gowns, she picked up the green muslin.

Nose scrunched, Justina mentally calculated, *again*, how long it took to travel to Lancashire and back while allowing a week for him to attend to whatever urgent business had required his attention.

Bristol was but thirteen miles from Bath. A trip he could easily make on horseback in an hour and a half, depending on how much he walked or galloped his mount. How naïve she'd been to think that some force beyond her or him had inexorably brought them together.

Lifting her dance slippers to place them inside the

trunk, a frown puckered her forehead.

Blister and blast.

A worn spot marred the sole of the right slipper. Running a fingertip across the leather, she pondered whether it would wear through during the house party. She checked the inside of the slipper, as well, grateful no holes were visible.

Giving a little shrug, she accepted the indisputable truth. It was too late to have the slipper repaired or order a new pair. She'd have to save them strictly for dancing and avoid walking about unnecessarily. Perhaps she'd even sit out several dances.

Pshaw.

Her hostess wouldn't permit it. Theadosia was renowned for making her guests feel at ease. No attendee to any of her events ever felt neglected or loitered by a wall.

In all likelihood, Justina fretted about nothing. No one would be looking at the soles of her feet, for heaven's sake.

After tucking the slippers into a corner of the trunk and adding nankeen half-boots and two other pairs of slippers, she permitted her contemplations to gravitate to Baxter once more.

As if she had any choice.

Like wild ponies, the dashed, stubborn musings galloped in that direction more often than not, despite her resolve that they do otherwise.

As Baxter had requested, Justina had left her address with Mr. Bixby, slipping it to him quietly before Aunt Emily had settled their bill.

"Mr. Bathhurst asked for my direction," she'd explained, trying and failing not to blush.

The dear man's eyes had twinkled behind his lenses, a kindly smile bending Mr. Bixby's mouth as he'd slipped the folded paper into a drawer.

"Rest assured, I'll see that he receives it promptly upon his return, Miss Farthington."

Justina had been a fool—*fool*—to believe Baxter.

I shall call upon you, Justina, when I return from Lancashire.

My intentions toward you are honorable. I vow it.

He'd seemed so sincere and earnest.

Believe me, please, he'd said.

And she had.

Ninny. Pea goose. Twiddlepoop.

Thank God, Justina hadn't given herself to him as she'd almost impetuously done. Would've done had he not drawn away. Never could she have imagined desire would carry her to the cusp of ruination and that she didn't give two farthings that it had. Even now, painfully aware that Baxter Bathhurst, the most handsome man—*the only man*—to upset her equilibrium didn't want her, caused heat to sluice through her.

It was humiliation washing over her— mortification at being dismissed and forgotten so easily.

Bah, what poppycock and tripe.

Justina snorted, refusing to lie to herself.

It wasn't embarrassment presently causing her blood to warm as it hummed through her veins. No indeed. It was the sweet, sensual memories of what Baxter had done to her. She'd wanted him to continue—to make her a woman in every way.

To make her *his* woman.

Why had he stopped?

Four words, an unwelcome mantra echoing in her mind, taunting and tormenting. Reminding her of her shortfalls.

That he was an experienced man of the world, Justina had no doubt. Perchance he'd found her lacking or repugnant in some manner. All that twaddle about calling upon her had been just that.

Rubbish. Balderdash and claptrap.

Had he only said he'd come to Bristol and knock upon every door so that he could make his escape that night without hurting her feelings?

Chagrin pricked Justina, sharp little jabs of self-castigation and recrimination further bruising her already battered pride. She grabbed the rose gown and carefully folded it before laying it in her trunk. At precisely nine of the clock tomorrow morning, she and Aunt Emily would depart for Colchester, a three-day journey.

Despite her vow that she'd not look for Baxter anymore, Justina's traitorous gaze wandered to the mantle clock and then veered to her bedroom window, which faced the street. A lone boy, head down and shoulders hunched against the drizzle, walked briskly along the lane.

No carriage drew to a stop outside.

No damp horseman trotted his mount to a halt.

There is still time, a little voice inside her head whispered.

He isn't coming, her logical self argued.

Stop looking for him. Cease torturing yourself.

Baxter had said he'd be done in Lancashire within a week. Even allowing time for travel, he should've been here by now. If he'd meant to keep his word.

Tears stung at the corners of Justina's eyes, and she scrunched them closed, refusing to give in to self-pity. She was not a watering pot.

No more crying.

One doesn't fall in love in seven days.

But that week at Bathhurst Hotel and Spa had been glorious. Baxter had been glorious.

Bah.

That nonsense was the fanciful stuff of childish fairytales and silly novels for even sillier women.

Gullible women who believed in love at first sight. Women who were guaranteed a broken heart.

She groaned and pressed her knuckles to her eyes.

Lord, she'd actually told Baxter that *she* believed in love at first sight.

And he'd promptly become acutely uncomfortable.

That should've clued her to his true feelings.

I don't love him, Justina stubbornly admonished herself. It was nothing more than girlish infatuation and an understandable physical response to a charming man well-versed in seduction.

Good God.

She dropped her balled hands to her sides, horror encompassing her.

Was wantonness another legacy from her disgraced mother?

Cringing at the thought—at what had become of Elsa Trattner as a result of her poor decisions—Justina reminded herself she ought to be grateful. Why, she might've found herself with child, just like her mother, and then what would she have done?

Aunt Emily didn't deserve that burden either.

No, Baxter's perfidy had cleared the stars from Justina's eyes and the cobwebs from her thinking. Too bad it hadn't curbed her physical yearnings.

That would come.

In time, Justina vowed.

She knew that to be the lie that it was.

Recalling the pitying glance Aunt Emily had given her during their midday meal today, which Justina had barely touched, she groaned aloud again.

"Foolish dolt," she mumbled to the open trunk.

Anxious that Aunt Emily would object, Justina had permitted nearly a full week to pass before she'd mustered the gumption to tell her aunt that Baxter would be calling upon her.

To her astonishment, Aunt Emily had only softly said, "I expected as much."

"How could you have known?" Justina had asked in astonishment.

She didn't dare share how he'd come to her room and what had transpired afterward, so she'd fibbed and said he'd asked her in the greenhouse the day Emily was indisposed.

"My dear," her aunt had said, laying aside her sewing, Justina's remade ballgown for the upcoming Christmastide house party. "You couldn't keep your eyes off one another."

Had everyone noticed?

Is that why Mr. Bixby's eyes had twinkled knowingly when Justina had slipped him the note with her address?

Chagrin singed her pride.

Aunt Emily had given Justina a long, probing look, faint tension evident in the lines bracketing her mouth.

"I would urge you to go slowly, Justina. Take your time and truly become acquainted with Mr. Bathhurst. You might think you suit now, but only time spent together will reveal the truth of that." She'd blushed prettily, her lovely porcelain skin turning quite pink. "Desire dies in the face of the unexpected and unforeseen."

At the time, Justina had thought the remark quite odd and, as usual, longed to ask precisely what Aunt

Emily meant. But a forlorn, stricken look had entered Emily's gaze, and Justina simply couldn't stand to cause her beloved aunt any more pain. So, she'd kept her question to herself. However, that didn't mean curiosity didn't burn within her.

Justina would've been wise to listen to her aunt's solemn advice. For she spoke from experience, but the giddiness that had previously spiraled through her was disinclined to wait.

More fool she.

Melancholy creasing the corners of her mouth and eyes, Aunt Emily had looked out the window, rain lashing the panes with angry, tear-shaped droplets. After a moment, she returned her regard to Justina once more. "I rushed into a marriage after a brief acquaintance. I was utterly convinced I was in love...and similarly positive that Clement loved me."

What had caused her to believe otherwise?

"What happened?" Justina asked softly, almost afraid to voice the question lest her aunt retreat into her usual silence on the matter.

Aunt Emily had only shaken her head and said,

"That's a tale for another time, my dear."

Pushing all thoughts of Baxter Bathhurst aside, Justina finished her packing and then went in search of her aunt. It was time to tell Aunt Emily that Justina had been mistaken about Baxter. He wouldn't be calling. She intended to put him from her heart and mind and to thoroughly enjoy her time at the Sutcliffes.

She might even flirt with the unmarried male guests.

Flirt?

Justina didn't flirt.

Well, wasn't there a first time for everything?

I shall never visit Bath again.

The unbidden thought intruded upon her reverie.

Codswallop.

If Aunt Emily could recover from what appeared to be a tragic, albeit short marriage, Justina most assuredly could square her shoulder, hold her chin up, and paste a smile upon her face for their dinner with Gertrude this evening.

For goodness sake. Justina had barely known Baxter, and seven days' acquaintance was assuredly inadequate to form a proper opinion about anyone, let alone an attachment. Yes, indeed, she'd learned a valuable lesson and thanked Providence she had not sacrificed her virginity for an unworthy scapegrace.

She'd not even leave word with their manservant, Fletcher Tambling, or his wife, Eunice, informing Baxter that she was away until the new year. No indeed. A man who couldn't be bothered to keep his word wasn't a man she was interested in furthering an acquaintance with.

You are a liar, Justina Farthington.

Bathhurst Hotel and Spa
Bath, England
16 December 1810

Baxter arrived home in the early morning hours, having pushed on to Bath despite his bone-deep weariness and Knight's fatigue as well. The loyal horse would've continued on until dawn had Baxter required it of the eight-year-old bay gelding.

Yawning widely, Baxter climbed from his rumpled bed before the clock had chimed seven. As exhausted as he'd been, his slumber had proved restless, and he'd awoken frequently, his mind turning over and over to Justina.

She'd been in his thoughts continuously.

How he'd missed her.

That impish twinkle in her eye and the curve of those perfect lips.

Over three long weeks had passed since he'd vowed to her that he'd call as soon as he returned to Bath. And by Odin's toes, he was a man of his word. In hindsight, he should've asked her for her address before he left her chamber that night. Then he could've written to her and explained his delay in Lancashire.

As it was, she might very well believe he didn't intend to keep his word, and he couldn't blame her. He only had three days to call upon Justina and convince her of his sincerity before he must leave for Essex and that confounded Christmas house party.

Baxter would cry off if he hadn't given his word he'd attend and if he didn't need to discuss a business venture with the Dukes of Westfall and Sheffield as well as James Brentwood. The Dukes of Kincade and Asherford had also indicated an interest in the investment, as had his countrymen, the Dukes of Waycross and Heatherston.

Baxter couldn't deny it was most convenient that the men would also be in attendance. Such an opportunity could not be dismissed. It saved him from running about all over England and Scotland to meet with them.

He chuckled, imagining all of the dukes in one place.

Seductive scoundrels, the lot.

Well, they had been until several of the former rakes had recently wed. Still, a dozen dukes, all assembled for a Christmastide house party. Surely, that must be some sort of record.

The Scots didn't celebrate Christmas, so Baxter had absolutely no idea what to expect. Besides, he'd been assured the only unmarried ladies attending were dear friends of the hostess, and not one was on the prowl for a titled husband.

The latter, Baxter found nearly impossible to believe.

Making short work of dressing, he grimaced as he tugged on a pair of polished boots awaiting him. Covered in travel grime, the pair he'd worn for the journey home lay where he'd tossed them the night before.

As he didn't retain a valet, Coyle or Perkins would have them gleaming by this evening, but he couldn't prevent a small stab of guilt at the unpleasant task before them.

As eager as he was to see Justina again, Baxter wouldn't appear at her door looking like he'd come straight from his travels. She deserved more respect than that, though he'd venture to guess she wouldn't mind in the least if he did.

No, Miss Justina Farthington wasn't full of bumptiousness, nor did she affect airs. Not once had he heard her blather on about insipid topics such as the weather or fashion, drop the names of people of position she might've met at one time or another, nor did she gossip incessantly as the Popkin sisters were wont to do.

Justina was even-tempered, keen-witted, and delightfully unpretentious. But of utmost importance, she liked Baxter for himself. It had been five years since a woman—a woman of marriageable age, he swiftly amended—hadn't gazed upon him with a calculating glint in her gimlet eye and a determined set to her mouth.

Just the mention of his ducal title in conjunction with his single status had women frothing at the mouth like rabid hounds. Egads, it was almost enough to make a grown man turn tail and run.

Straight back to Scotland.

In the dead of winter.

Never an enviable prospect.

As Baxter swiftly brushed his sandy blond hair into some semblance of order, a frown tugged his mouth downward at the corners. He supposed he'd have to meet with Bixby and make sure all was well with the hotel before heading to Bristol.

That was the responsible thing to do, and the additional delay oughtn't to annoy as much as it did. Why, since Justina Farthington had burst into his life, did duties and responsibilities—both things he'd previously thrived upon—seem too deuced inconvenient?

As it had turned out, his plant manager, Irving

Grassley, had grossly understated the issues at Baxter's Lancashire plant. By the time Grassley had notified Baxter, someone had been sabotaging the equipment on an almost daily basis for a fortnight.

If that weren't inconvenient enough, not only had half of the workers become severely ill with what turned out to be influenza, but the others were also afraid to work for fear of contracting what they termed "*The curse*."

A rather superstitious lot, according to Grassley, the laborers blamed the sickness which swept the factory on the newly hired, one-eyed engineer, his face and body severely scarred by an explosion years ago.

Baxter had retained Jerome Carnes himself, also a Scot and a bloody genius when it came to engines and machines. Soft-spoken and painfully conscious of his alarming appearance, Carnes avoided contact with other people to spare them the shock. Unfortunately, his avoidance only served to strengthen the groundless rumors that Jerome also dabbled in the dark arts, Grassley had reported.

In short, the buildings had sat silent for over a

week, despite Grassley's efforts to encourage the unaffected workers to fulfill their duties. Then a few of the more radical young pups had decided to take matters into their own hands and had set fire to Carnes's living quarters, hoping to drive him away. The flames had spread to other buildings, putting six families from their homes, including sixteen children.

Thank God the worst injuries were smoke inhalation and a few minor burns. One man had sustained more severe burns when he dashed inside his home for the third time to save the last of his six children: seven-month-old twin lasses.

Baxter had been so enraged upon learning of the recklessness of the four imbecilic youths who'd set the fires that his first instinct had been to throttle them within an inch of their lives. The reckless fools had been summarily dismissed without reference, though Baxter hadn't brought them up on charges as they'd deserved.

They'd been ordered to leave the community and never return. As it turned out, those rotters were also responsible for the equipment malfunction. That, too, had been an attempt to frame Jerome and see him dismissed simply because the man was scarred, and they were superstitious idiots.

After the displaced families and Jerome Carnes had been relocated to other accommodations, Baxter had assembled those workers well enough to attend a meeting. He'd very concisely and firmly stated his full confidence in Jerome and told the others if they were unhappy with his choice of an engineer, they could take their leave, and he'd provide them with a reference.

Any future murmurings against Carnes would result in termination, and anyone engaging in further acts of violence would be turned over to the magistrate. Hence, what Baxter had believed would be a relatively quick trip had turned into an exhausting three-week-long trial.

As he descended the steps in search of Bixby, his dogs prancing at his heels, he grinned. Today he'd see that green-eyed enchantress that had plagued his waking hours as well as his dreams each night. He couldn't recall the last time such anticipation had assailed him.

"Bixby!" He strode through the expansive entry, excitement and expectation quickening his pulse and step. He glanced at the mahogany longcase clock, imported from Dundee, and calculated how long his discussion with his manager might take as he debated whether to skip breaking his fast.

Devil take it.

Was he actually considering not eating to expedite his departure and his reunion with Justina?

A derisive smile quirked Baxter's mouth.

That was a first.

He'd become a besotted numpty. Skipping meals. Riding his faithful horse until they were both ready to drop. Wishing to rush his duties, all to see a woman he'd known seven short days. One magical, marvelous week had been long enough to realize she was a treasure he couldn't allow to escape.

"Welcome home, Mr. Bathhurst."

Beaming a sincere welcome, Bixby pushed his spectacles up his nose as he stood proudly behind the counter on the stool Baxter had ordered built for him.

"I trust all is well in Lancashire? We expected your return far sooner."

"Aye, unfortunately, ignorance and fear breed mischief, and circumstances in Lancashire proved a great deal more complicated than I'd anticipated." Hands on his hips, Baxter grinned and surveyed the spotless entry.

Duke and Princess had deserted him, going in search of their morning meal.

"Things are well here?"

Bixby dipped his head. "Yes, sir. We currently have seven guests, and I received word yesterday that another four will arrive this afternoon. We have reservations for an additional eleven. During your absence, seven and thirty have come and gone."

Not too bad during the winter months.

Not too bad at all.

Bixby straightened to his full height and tugged on his lapels, a shadow of unease pleating his broad forehead and crinkling the corners of his usual jovial features.

"Has something occurred?" Baxter asked, unease

prickling along his spine.

"Edie eloped with Becker eight days ago."

Not at all surprised, Baxter chuckled and scratched his eyebrow.

The maid and groom had been sweet on one another for months. Honestly, he'd expected an announcement sooner. "Why couldn't they simply have told you or me? I'd have let them retain their positions. I have no objections to married couples working in the same establishment."

It worked out well at his other ventures.

"So I tried to persuade them." Bixby darted a wary look toward the entry. "The real issue is Edie's father. Emmet Swern promised her to another, and he says you are to blame for her elopement. He's been by every morning for the past week, demanding to speak with you."

"Me?" Baxter arched a brow. "What have I to do with the matter?"

One of the local blacksmiths, Swern had a fondness for the bottle that adversely affected the quality of his work. What was more, he was obstinate and meanspirited. More than once, Edie had arrived at work with a bruise marring her cheek or sporting a cut lip.

When Bixby failed to answer, Baxter leveled him a stern look.

"Bixby? Why is he demanding to speak with me?"

Bixby cleared his throat, appearing distinctly uncomfortable. Normally unflappable under the most trying of circumstances, a distinct reddish hue crept from his neck and upward over his cheeks before disappearing into his hairline.

"Well, sir," he hedged, fiddling with something behind the counter and not quite meeting Baxter's avid gaze.

"Yes?" Baxter bit out, far sharper than he'd intended.

He nearly ground his teeth to powder at the servant's continued silence but checked his impatience. It wasn't Bixby's fault a siren with petal-soft skin and velvet green eyes called to him.

After a swift glance about the entry and his voice lowered to a discreet level, Bixby said, "It seems Edie was, ah,"—the man's face turned impossibly redder— "in the family way, and Mr. Swern believes you are the father."

Baxter went utterly still, absorbing the startling information before finally saying, "Is the man daft?" Nae, but foxed to his fleshy jowls? Aye, Swern was off his head. "Why would she abscond with Becker if I fathered her child?"

His elfin ears turning crimson, Bixby swallowed audibly. "As to that sir, Mr. Swern claims you forced yourself on his daughter. He is demanding compensation, or he'll make his accusation public."

Shite.

Emmet Swern was a sodding idiot. If he'd spoken to Bixby about his ridiculous demands, Baxter could guarantee half of Bath knew of the accusation by now.

Baxter, too, glanced at the hotel's entry.

Hellfire and brimstone.

He'd have to delay his departure until he put the blacksmith in his place and disabused him of his ludicrous misconception. That neatly answered the question about whether to stay for breakfast. Baxter supposed it was just as well. He could hardly arrive at Justina's with his stomach growling from hunger.

"I believe Miss Farthington left something for me?"

"Ah, yes." Obviously relieved at the change of subject, Bixby reached into a rectangular cubby, withdrawing several slips of paper. He swiftly thumbed through them. A frown drew his brows together. "Where did I put that?"

He opened a drawer and rummaged around inside.

"Hmm," he mumbled to himself. "That's odd. I swear I placed it with the other messages for you."

"Is something amiss?" Baxter kept his voice calm, but visions of banging on door after door after door in Bristol invaded his mind.

He swallowed a vile oath.

"No, sir. I'm sure it's here." Bixby never misplaced anything. He didn't even permit the maids to dust his desk. "Ah, here it is."

His relief evident, he procured a neatly folded rectangle and waved it back and forth.

"I hired a new maid to take Edie's place. She must've taken it upon herself to dust or organize my desk." His eyebrows snapped together. *A capital crime, indeed.* "I shall speak to her again."

Something near giddiness whipped through Baxter. "I'll be departing for Bristol after I break my fast and speak with Swern. When he arrives, have Coyle show him to my office, but do not leave the wretch alone in there. Given a chance, he'll rob us blind."

His thoughts already on Justina, Baxter turned in the direction of the dining room, hungrier than he'd realized until just now. If he weren't mistaken, he smelled tattie scones and sausage. Mrs. Felton was a priceless treasure. She always seemed to sense when he craved a taste of Scotland.

Heavy, uneven footfall sounded on the porch before the hotel's front door burst open. Emmet Swern plowed in, face flushed and fairly growling, "Ye're finally back, you bloody, ruttin' blackguard."

Baxter barely had time to turn around before

Swern was upon him, fury spewing from his eyes, the reek of strong drink radiating from every oversized, sweaty pore.

Distracted by his musings of Justina, Baxter blinked in surprise, then ducked too late to avoid the meaty fist that landed squarely upon his jaw.

Jesus and Joseph.

He flew backward, landing hard on his arse.

Outrage replaced his warmer emotions as he winced against the ache in his jaw. No doubt about it. The blow would leave a large bruise.

"I say," Bixby exclaimed, coming around the counter, prepared to defend Baxter, though he was a full two feet shorter than Swern.

Coyle and Perkins pounded in from the corridor, expressions fierce as each bolted to Baxter's side and took up defensive stances.

Growling, low in their throats, Duke and Princess pelted into the entry. Teeth bared, they hovered near the doorway, their black eyes fixed upon Swern.

"Sit," Baxter said.

The dogs obediently sank to their haunches, but their wary gazes flickered between him and Swern.

Touching his jaw, moving it gingerly from side to side to test if it was cracked, Baxter found his feet. Not broken but assuredly bruised. Swern was built like a bull and possessed the same obstinate, unpredictable temperament.

"If you leave now, Swern, I shan't have you brought up on charges," Baxter said slowly and deliberately, taking the man's measure.

"*Charges*?" Swern sneered, wiping his nose on the back of his soiled sleeve.

"You got me Edie wif child." Giving a hearty sniff, he clenched his ham fists again. "I demand recom...recom..." He stumbled over the unfamiliar word. "Recom-pen-see. She was to marry another."

Likely a decrepit or debaucher that Swern owed a favor. Or owed money. Mayhap both.

Nostrils twitching, for the blacksmith also stank of stale sweat and unwashed body, Baxter eyed the other man. He'd never liked him. Loud, arrogant, and opinionated, the sot bullied his wife, children, and neighbors. Half of his customers too, which was why he found himself with so few of them.

God's teeth, no wonder the couple had eloped.

"I never touched your daughter, Swern." Baxter never dallied with his female employees. To do so was an abuse of power and utterly contemptible. "If she was in the family way, then I'll wager Becker fathered the child. It was plain to see they were in love."

"Bullshite," Swern swore savagely, spittle clinging to the right corner of his mouth.

"I'll thank you to keep a civil tongue in your head, Swern," Baxter warned.

"I've lived in these parts the better part of four decades, Bathhurst. You've only been here for three years. Who do you think the locals will believe?"

Sanctimonious pizzle.

Swern puffed out his chest and jammed his hands into the pockets of his trousers, confident he had Baxter backed into a corner. "I'll keep me mouth shut fer five hundred pounds."

"That's robbery," Bixby gasped, looking from Baxter to Swern and then to Baxter once more. "And extortion." He peered up at Baxter. "Should I send for the magistrate?"

"No need." Baxter straightened his mussed waistcoat, then turned his steeliest stare upon Swern. "*If* I ever fathered a child, I would take full responsibility for it and ensure it never wanted for anything. But as I already said, I never laid a finger on Edie, and I'll wager she never suggested I did, either."

A guilty flush stole up Swern's already ruddy cheeks. He puffed them out, his mud-brown eyes narrowing menacingly.

The bugger likely wanted the coin for more whisky. And Swern would blackmail Baxter for the rest of his life if he paid a single crown now to bridle his loose tongue.

"Well, she's not here to say one way or t'other, is she?" Swern snarled. "So I suggest you pay up. Rumors are ugly things, Bathhurst." A smug smile contorted his mouth and fleshy, unshaven cheeks. He pulled on his ear as if imparting some great revelation. "They've been known to ruin a person's life. How many guests do you think would stay at yer hotel when word gets out that you violate yer female servants? Would any lady feel safe stayin' here?"

"Given your penchant for drink and your tarnished reputation, you really aren't very bright, threatening me." Baxter jerked his chin toward the door. "Leave now, and I'll forget this unpleasantness ever happened."

Swern swallowed, a glint of uncertainty flickering his scheming gaze.

"It's yer word against mine," he said, all belligerent bravado.

Bollocks to that.

Baxter had had enough.

Every minute he wasted talking to this drunkard was one that kept him from Justina and explaining his tardiness to her. He stalked closer to Swern, every step predatory as he struggled to keep his wrath in check until he stood directly in front of Edie's hostile father.

Baxter had the height advantage, but the squat blacksmith with cudgels for arms outweighed him by at least four stones.

Leaning down, Baxter enunciated each clipped word in perfect aristocratic English.

"No, you opportunistic cretin. It is the word of a pished blacksmith against the Duke of San Sebastian."

9

Ridgewood Court

Colechester, Essex England

22 December 1810

Ensconced in Ridgewood Court's expensively but tastefully decorated drawing room, Justina couldn't stop smiling between sips of simply divine India tea. Her dearest friends, Ophelia Breckensole, Gabriella, Duchess of Pennington, Jessica, Duchess of Bainbridge, Nicolette, Duchess of Westfall, and Rayne Wellbrook, surrounded her.

She'd sampled several exquisite dainties and biscuits, too, but resisted further indulgence. The excess of delicious foods and treats throughout the house party would have her gaining half a stone if she weren't diligent.

"I vow," Jessica said, patting her tummy as she sent her sister a fond look, "Thea's goal is to fatten all of us up."

As always, Theadosia had outdone herself. She positively adored entertaining.

Bows of greenery and holly, festooned with red, silver, and gold ribbons, adorned every room. Several kissing boughs and mistletoe twigs, those also beribboned, dangled from doorways inviting clandestine kisses. Clove oranges sat in crystal bowls, adding more delicious aromas to the already fragrant house.

The remaining guests would arrive this afternoon, and everyone but the late arrivals had gathered for tea this afternoon. Everyone would gather for dinner, however.

Across the room, several gentlemen, most of whom Justina knew quite well but a few she hadn't previously met, spoke animatedly about the horse race tomorrow. Quite magnanimously, they'd offered to allow any ladies who were up for the challenge to join them. The American heiress, Sophronie Slater, had boldly dared to wager she'd win the race.

Justina considered the vivacious strawberry blonde whom she quite admired. Sophronie just might do it. Surreptitiously so that Aunt Emily wouldn't catch wind of her brazenness, Justina had bet a whole pound yesterday that Sophronie would win. Such extravagance was unlike her, but everyone was betting against Sophronie.

Tobias Forsythe, Duke of Heatherston, had good-naturedly agreed to record the bets while Aunt Emily slid him disapproving sideways glances. She didn't hold with women racing about the countryside, riding astride in breeches as Sophronie was wont to do. Aunt Emily also frowned upon the current fashion of women gambling—any gambling for that matter.

Wasteful, frivolous behavior, she'd decreed.

As they'd never had the coin to spare for such frivolity, Justina felt very recalcitrant indeed. And not just a little guilty for keeping a secret from her beloved aunt.

Rayne caught Justina's eye and subtly rolled her eyes in Ophelia's direction. Their friend, teacup to her lips, avidly peeked at Stanford Bancroft, Duke of Ashford, from beneath her lashes. A slight crease drew her brows together, and it was impossible to determine whether his grace intrigued or peeved her.

Across the room, the Scottish Duke of Waycross scowled darkly at Sophronie while Aunt Emily studiously disregarded Heatherston, another Scotsman, sitting to her right. Most men, when given Aunt Emily's cold shoulder, hied on their way, and yet Heatherston glibly remained.

Either the man was obtuse, or he didn't mind.

Or perhaps, he was just stubborn and refused to let Aunt Emily have her way.

Had Aunt Emily met her match, at last?

Justina arched a speculative eyebrow.

Hmm, the next fortnight might prove very interesting, indeed.

Last year, Everleigh, Rayne's step-aunt, and Griffin, Duke of Sheffield, had fallen madly in love during the Sutcliffes' holiday house party.

Who knew?

Perhaps another young lady would find herself wedding her Christmas duke this year. There certainly were enough of their ducal selves in attendance that any young woman might find herself quite dizzy.

Fortunately, Justina's unwed friends were sensible girls, and they'd all spent enough time around peers that they didn't fawn all over themselves or make calf-eyes at eligible gentlemen.

For the benefit of their guests, and to cause less confusion with so many *his graces* and *her graces* in attendance, Theadosia had decreed that the duchesses would answer to their first names and the dukes to their titles.

Society might frown upon such intimacies, but most of these people were good friends, and other than number each duchess and duke, there was little help for it.

Another reason to avoid marrying a man with a title, Justina concluded with no small amount of satisfaction. She would happily settle for an honest, kind man of common birth.

A sandy-haired, honey-eyed Scottish hotelier?

Do be quiet, she chastised her troublesome inner voice.

That ship had sailed.

No, that ship had been scuttled and had sunk to the ocean's deepest depths with no survivors.

Yes, Justina affirmed to herself, she intended to marry a man who wouldn't care about her humble birth or her illegitimacy. A man who preferred living outside of London but didn't mind a visit or two to Towne each year. After all, she'd want to visit her dearest friends on occasion.

In truth, Justina hadn't quite decided whether to reveal the murky details of her past to her future husband.

Heavens.

Look at her. Contemplating marriage—something Justina hadn't seriously done before. But as there were no besotted beaus or enamored swains waiting in line to claim her hand, the decision could wait.

Mayhap would always wait.

A sliver of doubt wedged itself near her heart.

There it was again.

That annoying but undeniable truth.

There was no guarantee that she'd wed. In fact, the scales were weighted against the probability. After all, she hadn't a dowry. Aunt Emily had done well by Justina, but a dowry just wasn't manageable. Truth be told, spinsterhood wasn't that farfetched, nor was the notion abhorrent before this unexpected stop in Bath.

A hard, swift pang stabbed Justina's heart, leaving her breathless for a long, painful moment. She'd thought Baxter might be the man for her. Their attraction had been so swift and potent.

Plainly, not as potent for him.

Fine, she'd not have what she desired this Christmas, but sheer mulishness kept a cheerful smile upon her face.

Baxter Bathhurst would not taint her enjoyment, the insensitive, dishonest cad.

But he already has.

"Will you ride tomorrow, Justina?" Sophronie asked, her blue eyes alight with excitement.

The girl adored horses and was quite the most

accomplished horsewoman of Justina's acquaintance.

Justina shook her head.

"No, I've not spent enough time in the saddle of late to consider myself worthy." In point of fact, Aunt Emily didn't keep a saddle horse, and the only times Justina went riding was when they visited a friend. She sat a saddle well but was by no means accomplished.

"Rayne, will you?" Sophronie urged, hope making her eyes bright.

Rayne also shook her head, contrition in her unusual amber-brown gaze. "Regretfully, no. I've promised to help plan the parlor games."

Disappointment settled onto Sophronie's features, but she rallied a moment later and smiled her understanding. Poor dear. She might be the only woman daring enough to race with the men.

"Parlor games?" murmured the Duke of Heatherston, his Scottish brogue deep and melodic and perhaps tinged with a thread of hilarity. Or horror.

Justina wasn't sure which.

"Och, however shall I contain my glee?" he drawled, quirking a reddish eyebrow, a distinctly amused glint in his deep blue eyes. "What shall it be? Blind Man's Bluff? Hot cockles? The Aviary?"

Justina bit back a laugh.

Aunt Emily gave him an acrid glance meant to take him down a peg, which only produced an indolent grin. "Shan't *you* be racing neck for nothing, belly to the ground, with the others, Your Grace?" she said far too sweetly.

Justina barely kept her jaw from sagging at the fascinating exchange.

"Rest assured, everyone," Theadosia announced, having overheard the conversation and rushing in to diffuse any awkwardness. "There are plenty of activities for everyone's enjoyment."

True to form, the duchess would ensure her guests' pleasure—whether they liked it or not.

"More tea, Justina?" Nicolette asked, her gaze sweeping the room. Newlywed, there was no need to ask whom she searched for. As if sensing her perusal, Mathias, Duke of Westfall, shifted his regard from the Duke of Kincade and winked at his wife.

A pretty blush tinting her cheeks, Nicolette gave

him a beatific smile.

"*Ahem*. Yes, more tea would be wonderful," Justina said, hiding her smile.

Seeing Nicolette and their other married friends blissfully happy was a bittersweet sensation. As thrilled as Justina was for them—she truly wasn't so shallow as to be jealous—it served to remind her of what she stupidly believed she might have had with Baxter.

Even now, thoroughly disenchanted, her thoughts turned to him. She couldn't help but wonder if he'd arrived on her doorstep in Bristol after she'd departed for Colchester.

Had he been disappointed when she'd not been at home?

Had he inquired when she would return?

Was there a plausible excuse for his delay?

Wishful thinking, Justina.

Indeed. That was all any of it had ever been.

Aunt Emily was forever saying if wishes were horses, beggars would ride.

Wishes, dreams, fanciful expectations… All led to

disappointment and discontent.

"Ah, there you are, San Sebastian. I'd begun to wonder if you were going to make it after all," the Duke of Sheffield said. "I understand you've had troubles in Lancashire."

Lancashire?

Her back to the entry, Justina scrunched her eyebrows together, resisting the urge to gawk over her shoulder. She supposed it wasn't so odd that Sheffield's friend had business in Lancashire. The city was, after all, a hub for industry.

If she recalled correctly, Sophronie's father was also Sheffield's business partner.

"Word certainly travels fast." A droll chuckle accompanied the remark. "You are correct. There were issues with my textile factory that required my attention. However, everything has been set to rights now."

Justina froze, her nape hairs rising and her skin puckering like a plucked goose.

No. It cannot be.

She *knew* that voice.

She knew that delicious chuckle, as well.

Oh, God, please don't let it be him.

Christmas will be ruined. Ruined!

She almost shook her head to dislodge the ringing in her ears and heartily wished she'd not indulged in so many biscuits as her stomach felt rather wretched.

Aunt Emily gasped and coughed.

Or had she choked on a sip of tea?

Justina's gaze shot to her aunt.

Features strained, her aunt stared open-mouthed toward the other side of the room. Her delicate China teacup slipped from her fingertips, shattering on the floor and drawing everyone's attention.

That was all the confirmation Justina needed.

Bloody, bloody, maggoty hell.

Justina permitted her eyelids to drift closed for a heartbeat.

How could he have known where she was?

They hadn't left word with the Tamblings.

The truth struck her as painfully as a punch to her ribs.

Baxter *hadn't* followed her here.

He was an invited guest too.

Sutcliffe's comment should've alerted her, but in truth, she'd been so rattled upon hearing Baxter's voice that she could scarcely cobble a coherent thought together.

He doesn't know I'm here.

"Oh, dear. Do forgive me, Theadosia," Aunt Emily managed after marshaling her composure in a rather admirable fashion.

"I dropped a cup myself last week," Theadosia graciously assured her as she moved to the bellpull to summon a servant to see to the mess.

A hole.

Justina prayed the floor would open up—just a small opening—so she might slip inside before Baxter noticed her.

Baxter Bathhurst was not only Scottish, but the rapscallion was also the Duke of San Sebastian. He'd conveniently forgotten to mention *that* critical detail. Not once had he hinted that he held a title, *the rotter*. No wonder he'd failed to keep his promise. He'd been hiding a rather large secret.

He was a duke.

Just what this assemblage needed—another bloody duke!

Chagrin and anger and hurt all vied for dominance, swirling inside her, a maelstrom of emotions. Taking a deep breath, Justina strove for equanimity as she set her teacup upon the table with a steadiness that surprised but pleased her.

Tucking her fingers beneath her skirts, she curled them into claws.

Justina wanted to hit him.

Slap his handsome, arrogant face for making a fool of her—for so cruelly toying with her affections.

My God!

She'd kissed him. Allowed him unspeakable liberties.

Wonderful liberties.

Her blood burned hot at the intrusive memory, and shame wasn't entirely to blame.

"Justina, dearest?" Distantly, as if through a cloying haze, she heard Aunt Emily say her name.

How fast could Justina pack?

Could their carriage be readied in ten minutes? Five?

Forget packing. No time to waste.

The clothes on her back would suffice quite nicely.

She'd send for her things later.

Once Justina had escaped and her every breath wasn't labored and each heartbeat a lancing pain.

"Mrs. Grenville. What an unexpectant but pleasant surprise," Baxter said, that mesmerizing touch of brogue washing over Justina like sweet, warm chocolate.

Could one drown in chocolate?

Throat tight and lightheaded, she very much felt like she was drowning. Placing a palm on her ribcage, she felt the irregular cadence of her breathing.

In and out. In and out. That's it.

"And Miss Justina Farthington."

Was it her imagination, or had a possessive, caressing inflection entered the timbre of his voice?

Caressing?

Oh, my God, Justina. Collect your scattered wits and be gone.

"You are acquainted with his grace, Justina?" Ophelia asked the obvious question, two neat lines puzzling her forehead. The inquisitive glance she leveled Justina fairly shouted, *"You've been keeping secrets, Justina Farthington."*

Justina sent Nicolette and Rayne a desperate look.

Utter befuddlement was stamped upon their features. Of course, they'd help her in a blink if only they knew how.

Baxter—*blast his gorgeous eyes*—stood beside Justina now, and she couldn't help but notice the drawing room's excruciatingly lengthy and painful silence or that everyone keenly watched their stilted exchange.

"Only *very* slightly," Justina said, lifting her chin. "So slightly, in fact, to not count or be remarked upon at all."

So there. Make of that what you will, Your Grace.

"That is not my recollection," he replied silkily. "I

remember quite clearly, and it was *most* memorable."

Her friends' gazes bored into Justina as heat flamed across her cheeks.

Oooh, now Justina *really* did want to hit him.

To clobber him soundly—box his ears until they rang. To wipe that self-assured expression from his handsome face and the humorous glint from his knowing eyes.

Summoning every ounce of gumption she possessed, Justina slowly rose and met his probing gaze and those warm, tempting caramel-brown eyes.

One can definitely drown in caramel and not mind it in the least.

The inane thought only further fueled her wrath.

She shouldn't be noticing his eyes or his voice or the angles of his face. Nor the way his superfine black coat fit his ridiculously broad shoulders and chest to perfection.

And all the while, his gaze remained open and inviting.

She had no doubt, fury and betrayal sparked in her

eyes. Dipping into a curtsy that would've had the patronesses at Almacks applauding, she murmured, unable to keep the note of contempt from her tone, "Your *Grace*."

Scapegrace was more like it.

Codpated cabbage head.

Liar.

A monologue of much worse expletives marched along inside Justina's head. She'd save those invectives for the privacy of her bedchamber where she might pummel a pillow to perdition as well.

Betrayed. Wholly and utterly betrayed. Eviscerated.

The pain and humiliation nearly doubled her over.

And yet, she must hold her head up, keep her spine straight, and pretend as if everything in the universe was right. That her whole world hadn't just tipped off of its bloody axis. That the man standing so close to her that his essence drifted to her nostrils hadn't shredded her stupid, gullible heart.

The sweets Justina had so enjoyed earlier roiled in

her belly, and nausea crept up the back of her throat. Swallowing hard, she willed the contents of her stomach to remain where they were.

Theadosia might be the epitome of graciousness, but even she would be hard put to remain courteous should Justina cast up her accounts on the expensive Aubusson carpet.

"Please, excuse me." Mustering all of her composure, and with the aplomb of a queen, Justina swept past Baxter without another glance and made for the door.

"Justina?" Aunt Emily and Justina's friends chorused behind her, their voices a mixture of concern, distress, astonishment, and perhaps a tinge of curiosity too.

"Whatever is going on?" one of the men queried— she had no idea which, as her back was to the room. Bafflement riddled his tone

Perhaps it was one of those two fellows she'd never met before, the Earl of Keyworth or Kingston Barclay, the presumptive heir to another bloody dukedom.

Just as Justina grasped her ivory and ocean-blue skirts to pelt to her chamber like a wounded fox chased by zealous hounds, Baxter said, "I must speak with her."

Perfect. Reveal to all and sundry that there was something—*had been*—something between her and Baxter.

"*I. Think. Not!*" Aunt Emily clipped out, each syllable razor-edged, and her tone frostier than the Austrian Alps in January.

Indeed, he would not, Justina vowed, her teeth clamped to keep from spinning on her satin-slippered heels and telling him to go the devil.

"In fact, I absolutely forbid it," her aunt declared, which—*blast it to Hades*—would only serve to pique the interest of every person present all the more.

Justina's friends wouldn't rest until they had extracted every minuscule detail from her. And she simply could not share something so intimate.

Perchance she'd skip calling for a coach

altogether.

Yes, she'd fetch a horse from the stables. Mount the blasted thing and ride away astride, hell bent for nothing. Never mind her horsemanship, or lack thereof, would likely get her neck broken.

Wasn't there an inn three or four miles away?

Anything to avoid Baxter and the guaranteed inquisition she'd face from her friends if she didn't escape at once.

Something very near a growl of frustration reverberated in Justina's throat.

No. As much as she yearned to, she couldn't flee. Couldn't leave Aunt Emily to face everyone alone, more was the pity.

Her gown held indecently high, Justina took the stairs two at a time. She simply could not spend another second in the same room with Baxter and maintain her composure.

Once in her chamber, she locked the door before flopping onto her back onto the bed.

Oh, the cad.

The charlatan.

It had all been a lie. Everything.

The kiss. The caresses. The whispers. The vows.

She pounded the mattress.

Lies. Lies. All lies.

Turning onto her side, Justina pulled a pillow to her chest and tucked her knees up. Burying her face in the fine cloth, smelling slightly of honeysuckle, she let the tears come.

When, exactly, had she given her heart to a duke?

10

Baxter swallowed the oath tapping at the back of his teeth.

He could hardly dash after Justina without giving rise to unwanted speculation. He didn't know most of the guests beyond a mere acquaintance, and by juniper, he wasn't going to have anyone slinging mud upon her reputation. Although, to be fair, these people appeared more concerned for her welfare than bent on conjectures about what had just occurred.

The dinner gong pealed, and the Duchess of Sutcliffe motioned for her guests to precede her. After giving her adoring spouse a speaking glance and receiving a nod in response, she sailed directly toward Baxter.

Mouth pulled tight in censure, Mrs. Grenville stabbed him with an icy glare.

If looks could kill…

"I should check on my niece," she coolly informed

her hostess.

"Emily, I think perhaps, Justina needs time alone." The duchess curved her mouth into a sympathetic smile. "I shall have a tray and a bath sent up. A hot toddy as well."

Mrs. Grenville shot Baxter another venomous yet speculative glance, then tilted her head in agreement. "Perchance you are right, Thea. I'll speak with her before I retire."

Kingston Barclay approached, standing a respectable distance away so as to not intrude upon the conversation.

"I would be honored to escort you into dinner, Mrs. Grenville."

With another starchy glance at Baxter, she accepted Barclay's arm. Since neither held a title, they were amongst the last to go through to dine.

Her grace threaded her hand through Baxter's elbow and quite deliberately lingered until only they remained in the drawing room.

"Tell me, San Sebastian, how is it that one of my dearest friends has never mentioned you? But given her reaction of a few moments ago, I would venture you are more than slightly acquainted with Justina and her aunt."

More so with Justina.

Emily Grenville Baxter had scarcely had a conversation with.

When he'd arrived at their house a week ago and learned they'd left that very morning, he felt as if a draft horse had kicked him. He'd wanted to pummel Swern for delaying him. And when the closed-mouth servants refused to even hint at where Justina had gone so he might write to her, dual yokes of frustration and despair had settled upon him.

He'd nearly sent word to Sutcliffes that he wouldn't be able to make their gathering after all. But he'd managed to wheedle out of Fletcher Tambling—with the aid of several coins—that Justina wouldn't return home until the first of the year.

Baxter had been undecided whether to alert her to the servant's susceptibility to bribery but, on the journey, had decided against it. Tambling had kept his mistress's destination confidential and likely surmised, rightly so, that Baxter would return again *And again*. By telling him when Justina was expected home, the wily servant had put off having to deal with Baxter until that time.

"I'm waiting, Your Grace." The duchess wasn't having any of his delays, nor would she permit anything to upset her house party.

"I mean no disrespect, Your Grace, but I shan't discuss Justina with you." Baxter quirked his mouth into a sideways smile that a few ladies had claimed was charming. "Particularly not before I've had a chance to converse with her."

"Hmm." Her gaze shrewd and assessing, the duchess said, "My husband assures me you are one of the most decent men he has had the pleasure of not only doing business with, but with whom he is acquainted. If Victor trusts you, then so do I."

"But?" Baxter could see the challenge in her intelligent gaze.

"But, should you hurt Justina, or in any other way disrupt my holiday plans, you'll find I can be quite impossible."

He grinned. "Duly warned, Your Grace."

"Come along, then." She angled her head regally toward the doorway. "My guests are waiting."

The beautiful duchess promptly left his side when they entered the dining room and fairly floated to her end of the table. Once more, she met her husband's gaze, and sparks fairly flew between them.

And they weren't the only couple enjoying such intimate exchanges.

Rarely did the aristocracy marry for love, but from his brief observation this evening, each of the married dukes and duchesses present appeared to be the proverbial head over heels in love.

Rather than invoke Baxter's usual cynicism, the knowledge encouraged him.

When Justina had looked at him with such accusation and betrayal, he'd wanted to sweep her into his arms right then and there and beg her forgiveness and explain everything.

However, he had a distinct impression that she was livid because he was a duke.

Was there ever such a woman?

Tomorrow was far too long to wait to speak with her—to set things right between them. To apologize. If he had to pick the lock to her room, he'd do so.

Baxter found himself seated between Nicolette, Duchess of Westfall, and Ophelia Breckensole. Both women peppered him with questions about Justina, which he diverted by continually changing the subject or by asking them an unrelated question.

"You, sir, are deliberately steering the conversation away from Justina," Miss Breckensole accused with a merry twinkle in her eye. "Rest assured. Your evasiveness will do you no good, Your Grace. I shall have the whole of it from Justina sooner or later."

He'd only smiled and speared a piece of asparagus.

Never had a meal passed so excruciatingly slowly, nor the brandy and cigars afterward—each minute inching by.

Nonetheless, Baxter couldn't help but be impressed by the assembled men. Most were dukes save James Brentwood, Landry, Earl of Keyworth, and Kington Barclay. However, none of the aristocrats affected the arrogant air and haughty superiority he'd come to expect from English peers.

It also pleased him rather more than it ought to have done that other Scots were present as well. True, they were Scottish dukes, but it made him feel less of an oddity.

The men chatted like old friends, jesting and mocking, and despite the earlier scene with Justina, he found himself relaxing and enjoying their company.

Afterward, he tried not to gnash his teeth, roll his eyes, or sigh too often as various guests took turns at the pianoforte, some singing along and others strolling the room's perimeter.

What wouldn't he give to hear the pipes and enjoy an exuberant jig?

A dram of whisky wouldn't go amiss either.

Waycross caught his eye, and he swore the other man read his thoughts.

"I prefer the pipes, myself," he said, casting a furtive glance toward their hosts, who were singing a duet. "I may have brought mine and some Scotch too. I dinna ken how to celebrate Christmas, but

Hogmanay…? Aye, I ken what that is all about."

Mayhap during their stay, the Scots could teach the English a thing or two about Hogmanay and how the Scots celebrated the new year.

The clock chimed half-past ten.

Emily Grenville had departed forty minutes ago, insisting she needed to check in on her niece before she retired. Despite the young dragon's determination to keep him from Justina, Baxter meant to speak with her. Even if it meant climbing a lattice to Justina's balcony.

He checked the grin the image evoked.

He forced himself to wait until a few more guests bid goodnight before he begged exhaustion. He took his leave, mindful of a few raised eyebrows and swiftly exchanged glances from those remaining, not the least of which was his hostess's.

Hours ago, after using the excuse of needing the necessary, he'd casually inquired after Justina's health to a passing maid. The talkative servant also happened to be quite informative.

The slightly buck-toothed girl had grinned,

shoving several strands of light brown hair beneath her cap.

"She didn't eat much of her dinner, Your Grace. But after a bath and a hot toddy, Miss Farthington is right as rain. I made certain myself that her balcony doors were shut tight, her grate was full of coal, and I laid an extra blanket on the bed so she wouldn't catch a chill. When I left her, she was drying her hair before the fire. Her room is only three doors down from yours."

He'd rewarded the loquacious, slightly obtuse servant with a crown. She should never have revealed the location of Justina's room to him.

"Anything you need, Your Grace," she'd beamed. "You just ask Hannah." She jabbed a thumb at her less than ample chest. "I'll be happy to assist you."

It wasn't until he was halfway back to the drawing room that he realized the girl hadn't once batted her eyelashes at him or thrust out her bosoms. Likely, the Duchess of Sutcliffe took particular care to assure her staff had no aspirations of bedding her house guests.

Baxter would wager her grace had no idea just

how helpful Hannah was, however

Another hour and a half passed before the manor settled into the serenity of a slumbering house. He'd be daft to think everyone had already fallen asleep, but given it was already nearly midnight, he didn't wish to delay any longer. He'd shucked his boots and jacket upon entering his room and had nursed a glass of brandy while staring at the capering fire.

Justina might already be asleep, and he didn't want to frighten her.

Devil take it, who was he trying to fool?

His motivation was purely selfish.

He needed to see her.

Needed to explain and set things right between them.

Feeling very much like a thief in his stocking feet, he rapped upon her door.

"Justina," he whispered. "It's Baxter. I need to speak to you."

His mind flashed back to The Bathhurst Hotel when he'd done this very thing. That night she'd opened the door, and he'd tasted her berry-pink lips.

Tonight, only silence greeted his attempt.

He rapped again, casting a guarded glance up and down the corridor.

The last thing he needed was to be caught.

Still nothing.

He rested his forehead against the door and sighed.

"I'm sorry, *leannan*. I should've told you I was a duke," he murmured to the stout wood panel. "I vow, I'll make it up to you."

To his astonishment, the door opened six inches, as if Justina had been standing on the other side, listening.

Soulful green eyes gazed up at him, and his stomach clenched.

He'd done that to her.

"I couldna stay away," he said, slipping into Scots. "I had to make it right between us."

"I only opened the door to tell you to leave me alone, Your Grace. There can never be anything between us. You should've told me straightaway you were a duke, and I would never have allowed you to kiss me." She glanced away, bright color skating up her silky cheeks. "Good night."

"Wait, Justina." Baxter jammed his foot in the door, wincing as the wood pinched his toes. "I can explain."

She shook her head, her expression desolate. "Can you *not* be a duke?"

"What?" The question took him aback. "Of course not. But I care for you. *Deeply*."

By God. He might very well love her. *Did* love her.

The truth of that epiphany struck Baxter with such force, his breath and pulse stalled before resuming at an alarming pace. He loved Justina Farthington with her gorgeous eyes the color of his beloved Scotland. Each time he gazed into them was a homecoming.

"Then this is goodbye, Baxter."

A nascent smile, sad and fragile, curved Justina's mouth.

"I mean to convince my aunt to leave on the morrow, and I doubt you and I shall ever see each other again."

11

Early the next morning, her head aching from lack of sleep and the tears she'd wept after a stricken Baxter had backed away, permitting her to close and lock her bedchamber door, Justina went in search of her aunt.

She knocked thrice upon Aunt Emily's door and, after a long moment that stretched out into the corridor, received a groggy, "Who is it?" in response.

"It's me, Aunt Emily. I need to speak to you before the others arise."

After a bit of shuffling around inside, her aunt opened the door. "Come in, my dear."

"Forgive me for waking you."

Emily looked Justina over from head to toe.

"You've looked better, I must say. Did you sleep at all?"

No.

"As I'm sure you can imagine, I found slumber elusive," Justina admitted dully.

After yanking the bellpull, her aunt urged Justina into an armchair, then threw open the draperies. "I cannot stand drawn curtains when the sun is coming up. Light is healing, especially morning light."

Justina managed a wan smile.

"Now pray do tell, what has you dragging me out of bed at...?" Emily glanced at the bedside clock, her eyes going wide. "Merciful heavens," she exclaimed. "At half-past six?"

Justina folded her hands and met her aunt's eyes directly. "Can we go home this morning?"

"I take it, my dear, that you haven't looked outside?"

Justina shook her head.

"Darling, it snowed heavily overnight. Even if I believed we should depart, we cannot."

Despair gripped Justina, and then her aunt's words

caught her attention.

"You don't think we should leave? Why not? Baxter lied to me, Aunt Emily. He's a *duke,* and you and I both know there cannot be anything between us."

Her aunt angled her head. "I'll admit I was quite miffed with him last night, but upon further reflection, I believe you should give him the chance to explain himself."

Justina's mouth sagged, and she blinked several times in confusion.

"You...?" She shook her head again. "I don't understand."

A brisk knock echoed at the door.

"Come in," Aunt Emily called, securing the belt of her night robe at her trim waist.

"You rang, Mrs. Grenville?" A pretty maid with big blue eyes asked.

"Hot chocolate for my niece and me, please. And croissants and hot cross buns if they are available. The duchess's cook always makes the most delicious croissants."

"Of course." The maid bobbed a curtsy and left.

"Now, where were we?" Aunt Emily settled into the other armchair. "Ah, yes, his grace."

She chuckled as she put a forefinger to her chin. "I knew there was something about him I should recall. Remember when we first arrived at Bathhurst Hotel and Spa, and I said Bathhurst sounded familiar?"

Nodding, Justina strove to understand what her aunt was going on about.

Aunt Emily laughed again. "I remembered last night, and I must bear part of the blame for this situation. He attended the Duke of Westfall's ball last spring."

He had?

"I didn't meet him, of course, for I surely would have remembered him." Her aunt cocked her head, her eyes slightly squinted. "I believe I overheard that unpleasant Lady Crustworth complaining to her crony, Lady Darumple, that a Scot should never be permitted to inherit an English title."

"Be that as it may, Aunt Emily, that doesn't change the fact that Baxter wasn't honest with me, and he did not call as he'd promised to. And then there's me." Justina waved a hand toward her midriff. "I'm illegitimate. A nobody. Definitely not duchess material."

"Justina Madalene Honoria Farthington. I take great exception to that last statement."

"I'm sorry, Aunt Emily. I meant no offense."

Her aunt drew herself up, hurt etched upon her pretty face and shadowing her forest-green eyes. "I have taken extraordinary care to raise you in the manner of a most proper, gently-bred young woman. You *are too* duchess material. More so than most of the blue-blooded aristocrats I've met."

Turning her attention toward the window, Justina sighed.

It was snowing again.

Of course, it was.

Was God determined she should always be stranded in the same house as Baxter?

"Justina, may I ask you something personal?"

Justina veered her focus to her aunt once more. "Of course."

There'd never been secrets between them.

Well, except for the reason behind Aunt Emily's silence regarding her marriage.

"Do you love San Sebastian?"

The words were soft and empathetic and, yes, probably very hard for her wary aunt to ask.

"I do. I truly do." Swallowing, Justina battled the sudden swell of tears behind her eyelids. "So much so that I don't know how I can face the future without him."

Her aunt came to her then and crouched before her, taking her hands in hers.

"Darling, then tell him so. That man is in love with you. I'd wager everything I own upon it."

Justina studied her face, unable to deny the sincerity stamped upon Aunt Emily's features. "How can you, who won't even talk about what happened in your marriage, advise me on love?"

Hurt flashed across her aunt's face before she schooled her features once more. After taking a deep breath, she met Justina's gaze and clasped her hands tighter.

"I was in love once. Very much so. Clement

vowed he loved me too. We were married after a whirlwind courtship, and we were blissfully happy for two months."

Justina longed to ask what had happened but forced herself to wait patiently. She instinctively knew there was no rushing the telling of this tale.

Going pale, Aunt Emily looked away and bit her lower lip. After a long pause, she continued, her words strained.

"But, you see, my dear, he was already married."

Justina couldn't suppress her outraged gasp.

"His wife was in England with their three children. Clement received his new orders and promptly began packing to leave. I assumed he'd send me home to England to await him. When I asked him what arrangements I should make, he finally told me the truth."

"The heartless, rotten bounder." To have hurt Justina's sweet aunt in such a callous fashion was unforgiveable.

Aunt Emily managed a rueful, heartbreaking smile. "Oh, he swore he loved me, that his wife was a cold, unfeeling woman, but he had his children to consider, you see."

"Oh, Aunt Emily."

No wonder Emily had no interest in marrying again.

"He was killed shortly thereafter." A melancholic, nascent smile pulled her aunt's mouth upward. "I never even told my brother the truth. I was too ashamed, and Richard was a stickler for propriety. I honestly feared he'd turn me out."

With a bent knuckle, she wiped a tear from the corner of her eye.

That made Justina rather grateful Richard Farthington was not her sire. Or if he had been, as her grandfather had sworn that he was, that Justina had never known him.

"But you dear, what you have with San Sebastian. It's beautiful." Emily gave a tiny, self-conscious laugh. "I confess, I was envious. I didn't want to lose you. Or to be alone."

"I would never leave you!" Justina exclaimed, throwing her arms around her aunt's shoulders. "After all that you've done for me? How could you even think it?"

Aunt Emily gave her a tight hug in return and then a little shove. "Go, darling. Tell San Sebastian how you feel."

"I don't know which room is his." Giddiness tumbled around Justina's middle.

Could she really do it?

Proclaim herself?

Could she trust this feeling that had taken control of her life?

"Three doors down from yours."

Was her model-of-decorum aunt honestly telling her to visit a gentleman's bedchamber?

"I do believe I shall," Justina said, her courage growing with each word.

What had she to lose but the man she loved?

After kissing her aunt on the cheek, Justina hurried from the room, wishing she'd worn a different gown other than her slate gray and navy-blue traveling ensemble. She retraced her steps, this time her heart light and full of hope.

Justina would listen to what Baxter had to say. Hear what he'd wanted to tell her last night. She'd not throw away a chance for happiness because of her wounded pride.

A few moments later, she stood outside his chamber.

Ponies and puppies and all manner of creatures frolicked about her middle.

Drawing in a steadying breath, she knocked upon his door, one soft rap.

"Baxter?" She knocked again, a mite harder this time. "Are you awake?"

He threw the door open at once. After poking his damp head out and searching up and down the corridor, he swiftly drew her inside.

"Is something amiss, Justina?"

He wore only a towel about his waist, as if he'd come straight from the bath.

She wanted to throw herself into his arms, to tell him she was sorry she'd been so mulish and hardheaded. To kiss the vast, tempting expanse of his sculpted flesh. To do much, much more, in truth.

Instead, she gawked rather indelicately.

But, God above, he was gorgeous.

It truly was a crime that the Almighty had fashioned such a perfect specimen of manhood, and all of that male beauty was hidden beneath clothing most of the time. And though she ought to have blushed as any properly bred young woman would've done, she couldn't feign false modesty.

"Ah, no. Not precisely. Aunt Emily said I should speak with you."

A sandy-brown brow arched in bemusement. "Your *aunt* advised you to seek me out?"

"Indeed." Justina forced her attention from his exquisite physique, her focus landing on the bathtub and the tendrils of steam floating upward.

"Oh, you're bathing." She angled toward the door. "I'll come back later."

"No, please stay." Baxter turned her to face him. "What is it you wish to say?"

Her traitorous gaze crept to the damp mat on his chest, the shade slightly darker than the slicked-back locks upon his head. The tawny curls trailed downward in a tempting, teasing vee until it disappeared into his towel.

Was there ever such a perfect muscled and sculpted, masculine work of art?

Even the pinkish scars lashing his right shoulder and slicing across his ribcage didn't detract from his male perfection.

Justina's mouth had gone unaccountably dry. She swallowed, hauling her attention back to his face with considerable effort.

A smoldering glint of appreciation shone in his eyes. *Lion's eyes.* It suddenly dawned on her. That was what they were.

A sliver of uncertainty pierced her. "What did you want to say to me last night?"

"I'm sorrier than I can say, Justina, that I didn't tell you I was a duke."

Baxter cupped her shoulders, staring intently into her eyes as if willing her to believe him.

"Honestly, I've never liked the title, and in the five years since I inherited the dukedom, I've had women throwing themselves at me, wanting to be my duchess. I've chosen to not use the title except when in London or at gatherings where people already know who I am."

"It wasn't because I'm not nobly born?" Justina had to ask him, and at that moment, she acknowledged she must tell him the shameful rest as well.

There would be no more secrets between them.

He drew her to him, caressing her back and dropping tender kisses upon her head.

"Nae, lass."

His burr wrapped itself around her, seductive and tantalizing, and she loved that he felt comfortable enough with her to speak Scots.

"I care nothin' about yer birth. It's ye I love. Ye with yer impossibly green eyes that remind me of my beloved Scotland. With yer hair, the rich color of molasses, and yer red lips sweeter than any honey I've ever tasted."

"You love me?" Awed, Justina traced her fingertips across his freshly shaven jaw. "Truly, Baxter?"

"Aye. My heart is full of ye, Justina. Since the

moment I laid eyes on ye, my soul kent we were meant to be together. With ye, I am whole. Complete in a way I dinna feel when we are apart."

"Why didn't you come to Bristol?" Her voice broke. "I waited and waited."

And waited.

Her heart breaking more with each passing day.

She searched his dear face, adoring the slight wrinkles at the corners of his eyes, the sharp slice of his nose, his granite jaw. There was nothing soft about this man except for the expression in his eyes.

"Things were a tangle in Lancashire." Baxter tipped his mouth into a wry smile. "I had mechanical issues, rebellious workers, and sickness had gripped half of them as well. I should've asked for yer direction that night I came to yer bedchamber."

As he spoke, he caressed her, teasing butterfly sweeps of his fingertips that stoked the fire already smoldering in her blood.

"I went to see ye within hours after returnin' home, but yer servants wouldna tell me where ye'd gone."

"I was angry and didn't tell them where we were off to, only when we'd return," she admitted. "Though, I honestly didn't believe you'd actually come."

"I told ye once before, Justina Farthington. When I set my mind to somethin', I willna be dissuaded." He pressed his firm lips to her forehead, the gesture so sweet it brought tears to her eyes.

"Marry me, Justina. By special license or we can elope to Scotland. Say ye'll be my wife, my partner, and my helpmate."

He hadn't said duchess.

Because it didn't matter?

Or because it did?

Justina leaned away, bracing herself for what she must tell him.

"Baxter, there is something you need to know about me."

"What is it?" He grinned, the smile holding the promises of a lifetime with him. "That ye've stolen my heart? Me, who didna believe I would ever fall in love? That ye like feedin' the birds I rescued? That ye're almost as fond of honey as I am?"

Shaking her head, Justina giggled. "No to all of those. Although, I do want to hear how you came to have so many birds someday."

No sense in prevaricating about her history, however.

"I am illegitimate, Baxter. I may not even really be Emily's niece."

In short order, Justina told him an abbreviated account of her birth and coming to England.

For a pregnant moment afterward, he was totally silent, his expression inscrutable. Then he hitched his deliciously wide shoulders and quirked his mouth into a sideways smile.

"I dinna think I've ever met a woman as unselfish as yer aunt," he said. "If ye like, she will always have a home with us, although she's still quite young. She may very well marry again."

Justina shook her head. "I honestly don't think she will. She was terribly hurt by her first husband."

Perchance she'd tell Baxter that story someday. But not today and not without Aunt Emily's permission.

He hadn't directly addressed Justina's illegitimacy either.

"Baxter, I am the illegitimate daughter of an Austrian commoner. *You* are a duke. People will talk, and that's without knowing my tainted background."

His beautiful mouth bent into a bone-melting smile.

"*I* dinna care, lass, and that's all that matters."

Tears prickled behind her eyelids, and in that moment, she fell impossibly deeper in love with him.

"Ye didna answer me, Justina."

Baxter began removing the pins from her hair and, once it was free of its moorings, ran his fingers through the length. "I've longed to do this since that first day I saw ye sittin' in Bathhurst Hotel and Spa's drawin' room.

She threaded her fingers through his thick mane, the hair silkier than she'd ever have guessed.

"As have I," she admitted, thrilling at the low growl in his throat.

"Will ye marry me, love? I think I have loved ye from the moment ye said ye believed in love at first sight. Only I was blind to the truth right before me."

"I love you too, Baxter. I knew I did when you throttled Howlette on my behalf. And yes. I shall gladly marry you."

"Thank God." His lashes swept downward for an instant.

Justina cupped his face and pressed a long kiss on his mouth. "I get my wish, after all."

"Yer wish?" Baxter grazed a finger across her jaw, curiosity dancing in his gaze.

"I am to wed my very own Christmas duke."

Baxter pulled her into his arms. "Nae, lass. Ye are marryin' the man who will adore ye for the rest of our lives."

About the Author

USA Today Bestselling, award-winning author COLLETTE CAMERON® scribbles Scottish and Regency historicals featuring dashing rogues and scoundrels and the intrepid damsels who reform them.Blessed with an overactive and witty muse that won't stop whispering new romantic romps in her ear, she's lived in Oregon her entire life, though she dreams of living in Scotland part-time. A self-confessed Cadbury chocoholic, you'll always find a dash of inspiration and a pinch of humor in her sweet-to-spicy timeless romances®.

Explore **Collette's worlds** at
www.collettecameron.com!

Join her **VIP Reader Club** and **FREE newsletter**.
Giggles guaranteed!

FREE BOOK: Join Collette's The Regency Rose®
VIP Reader Club to get updates on book releases,
cover reveals, contests, and giveaways she reserves
exclusively for email and newsletter followers. Also,
any deals, sales, or special promotions are offered to
club members first. She will not share your name or
email, nor will she spam you.

http://bit.ly/TheRegencyRoseGift

Dearest Reader,

Thank you for reading WEDDING HER CHRISTMAS DUKE! I'm always delighted when a reader finishes a book I've written. It warms my soul.

For those of you skeptical about love at first sight, such as Justina and Baxter experienced, scientific studies have proven the phenomenon does exist. Interestingly, many of those who fall in love almost instantly and marry have remained married decades later. I personally know of multiple instances, including myself. My husband asked me to marry him after two weeks, and at the writing of this letter, we've been married thirty-nine years.

You can read the first chapter of all of the Seductive Scoundrels books and my six other series on my website. HOW TO WIN A DUKE'S HEART, Sophronie Slater and Evan Gordonstone, Duke of Waycross's story and THE DEBUTANTE AND THE

DUKE, Rayne Wellbrook and Fletcher McQuinton, Duke of Kincade, are next in the Seductive Scoundrels Series. And yes, Aunt Emily does find love. I bet you can guess who her hero is after reading this story.

Please consider telling other readers why you enjoyed this book by reviewing it. Reviews help an author so much.

Hugs,

Collette Cameron

The Debutante and the Duke

Seductive Scoundrels Series Book Eleven
A Historical Regency Romance

💙 **All she wants is her freedom.**

All he wants is her… 💙

Rayne Wellbrook shouldn't be living in a luxurious London manor. She shouldn't be the step-niece to a powerful duke, either. And she most certainly shouldn't be sneaking into the neighbor's gardens— even if the house is unoccupied. Or so she thinks until a rakishly handsome Scot startles her one morning. 😲 Though she's wary of men and even leerier of nobles, this man with his too-long hair and piercing blue-green eyes sends her heart 🖤 to frolicking. When he insists on an introduction, Rayne flees but can't get the enigmatic new neighbor out of her thoughts. 💬

Fletcher McQuinton, Duke of Kincade, is only in London long enough to put the finishing touches on his new business ventures, and then he intends to head straight back to Scotland. His meddling English mother has other plans, however—namely finding him an appropriate blue-blooded wife to become the next duchess. Fletcher has vowed to never take an English aristocrat as a wife, but when he comes upon a delightfully intriguing woman climbing his garden wall, he begins to reconsider his reluctance.

Can two polar opposites who are so perfectly wrong for each other overcome all that stands between them? Only one thing is certain. The road to happily ever after is about to get very bumpy...

THE DEBUTANTE AND THE DUKE

Seductive Scoundrels Series, Book Eleven

1

17 Bedford Square

London, England

2 June 1810

Singing softly, Rayne Wellbrook gently swung the heavy wicker basket she held. She skirted the fountain burbling in the center of the paved circle bordered by a quartet of stone benches in her aunt and uncle's elaborate gardens.

Between each ornate bench, marble statues of Greek goddesses and gods stood as majestic, silent guardians. Ribbons of morning sunlight cast them in luminous golden hues and gave each an ethereal appearance.

"I sow'd the seeds of love," Rayne sang a little louder.

"And I sow'd them in the spring,

"I gather'd them up in the morning so soon…"

Mama had been an opera singer until she married Papa and had instilled a love for singing in Rayne from the time she was able to speak. Mama and Grandmama had been gone for nine years now—Papa far longer.

Rayne couldn't even remember her soldier father.

Closing her eyes for a long blink, she filled her lungs with the sweet fragrances of jasmine, peonies, roses, and other vibrant summer blossoms festooning the zealously maintained pathways. Patches of lush green grass complemented the fastidious flower beds—each diligently attended by the cheerful gardeners the duke employed.

Mostly cheerful, that was.

All except for the fussy, meticulous head gardener.

Heaven forbid that Fitzroy—the surly curmudgeon—should find a single insolent weed or impertinent spent blossom amongst *his* beloved lower beds. The wizened, stoop-shouldered man even groused when the *"deuced impudent birds"*—his words, not Rayne's— used *his* fountains as birdbaths.

In point of fact, he objected when they used the birdbaths as *birdbaths*.

At present, a pair of bluish-black feathers floated in the middle layer of the fount's rippling water. Those avian offenders bespoke an early morning dip by a cheeky crow or raven, as the otherwise pristine water was too deep for smaller birds.

Chuckling, Rayne imagined the forthcoming scene.

Assuredly, Fitzroy would get *his* feathers ruffled as soon as he spied the evidence the trespassing birds had left behind. A string of colorful expletives would fill the fragrant air. Especially when he noticed the disrespectful droppings currently marring Zeus's noble head and impressive shoulders.

Fitzroy would gripe and scold while suggesting

several inspired ways in which to dispose of the feathered interlopers. Then he'd promptly send a younger, more agile gardener up a ladder to restore Zeus's tattered dignity.

Rayne plucked the feathers from the fountain—a small act of kindness. She'd dispose of them near the garden's back border.

For all of Fitzroy's crotchetiness, he allowed Rayne to snip yellow roses—her favorite—and other blossoms for her bedchamber bouquets as he stood by beaming and nodding like a proud papa. On numerous occasions, he'd even pointed out which blooms were at their peak.

Grinning, Rayne clasped her dark green and peacock-blue skirts and sank into a mock curtsy before Athena, the goddess of flowers. The translucent sunbeams flickering through the branches almost made it seem as if the statue winked at her.

As Rayne had absolutely no idea about the manner in which one should address a marble deity, she simply said, "Good morning, Athena."

A grating cry rent the air, and she glanced upward.

"And good morning to you too, Theopolis," Rayne quipped to the cheeky jay that had landed upon Apollo's head and expectantly stared at her with his tiny black eyes. Shading her own eyes, she tilted her bonnetless head, her unbound hair swinging across her back and shoulders. "Isn't it a lovely day?"

The bird made a soft but shrill sound.

"Patience, Theopolis."

In truth, she didn't know if the bird were male or female. Or, in fact, if it was the same flirtatious bird that greeted her nearly every morning. The pinkish-brown jay with its distinctive blue-and-black striped wing markings dipped its little head as if in agreement, waiting for the bread scraps she often brought with her.

She reasoned it must be the same bird since it made a habit of greeting her. And she decided, basing her assumption on the human species, that only a male would flirt so brazenly in hopes of getting a reward.

Reaching into her basket, Rayne located the stale bread and cinnamon bun she'd found in the kitchens when she'd pilfered a bite to eat for herself this morning. Nothing fancy, but enough to keep her stomach from growling as she read and sketched the morning away: a couple of rolls, a piece of yellow cheese, grapes, an apple, a jar of lemonade, and ginger biscuits.

Her purloined stash might very well last her until tea this afternoon.

"Here you are, Theopolis."

She tossed a piece of dried crust onto the ground.

With a strident cry, the jay swooped down, snatched the treat with his beak, and flew away. In his wake, a clouded yellow butterfly drifted toward the periwinkle-colored scabious, no doubt to enjoy sweet nectar for breakfast.

Rayne made a mental note to try to sketch the next clouded yellow she saw feeding. Doing so would test her artistic abilities, but she enjoyed challenging herself. Shouldn't one want to continually improve in some small way?

Spinning in a small circle, she sighed contentedly.

This was simply lovely.

Summer was her favorite season and morning her preferred time of day.

She'd awoken early, as was her custom, despite not having sought her bed until well past midnight. The ball hosted by her Aunt Everleigh and her husband, Griffin Dalton, Duke of Sheffield, last night had been a veritable crush and, therefore, a roaring *haut ton* success.

At least three hundred of *le beau monde's* finest had attended, ensuring write-ups in all of the gossip rags and newssheets that were of any account. Yes, the ball had been a rousing triumph. And made more so because her dear friend, Nicolette Twistleton, had received a very romantic, very sigh-worthy public marriage proposal from Mathias Pembroke, Duke of Westfall.

To Rayne's utter delight, Nicolette, who'd been previously jilted and had sworn off all men, had said yes.

Now Rayne and their other closest mutual friends were excited to congratulate Nicolette again and to hear all of the delicious details over several cups of steaming tea while nibbling decadent dainties, cakes, pastries, and biscuits.

Rayne was a debutante this Season—albeit a rather older debutante. Last night, she had danced several times and enjoyed a few splendid hours with her friends. Though in general, large gatherings inevitably strained her nerves.

A long-ago, disquieting memory tried to impose itself upon her current happiness. Rayne wasn't having any of that today. Purposefully tamping down the unpleasant recollection, she unceremoniously shoved the unsolicited remembrance into a distant corner as she'd learned to do over the years.

Nothing would ruin this delightful morning.

Today no heavy haze of coal dust layered the city, and the air was fairly fresh for London. The sky shone vivid blue for a change, with only a few wispy clouds feathered across the far horizon. Several birds' calls echoed from the trees and shrubberies in Griffin's illustrious grounds and also the less formal gardens next door.

Resuming her song, Rayne continued on the meandering footpath, each footfall a satisfyingly crisp *crunch* on the gravel.

"In June there was a yellow rosebud..."

Headed toward the farthest corner of the garden, she touched a fingertip to a velvety sun-colored rose as she passed by. On that side of the grounds, a stone wall, inlaid with small, projecting steps on both sides, separated the Sheffields' gardens from their neighbors'.

Neighbors who hadn't been in residence in a very long while, according to Griffin. Since before he'd purchased this stately house, in fact. And neighbors who, at one time, must've been close friends with whoever had owned the manor before Griffin.

For, why else would the stairs permit easy access across the wall if that were not the case? Perchance the residents of the two households had been relatives. She would have to remember to ask Griffin about that.

Mayhap he knew the history of the empty house and its owners. Or perhaps he knew if and when the absentees were expected to return to London. In the meanwhile, Rayne fully intended to continue enjoying the cozy fairy-like garden with its utterly delightful stacked-stone folly.

Did Griffin or Everleigh know about the steps in the wall?

Probably not, and Rayne wasn't positive that she wanted to share her secret. After all, she was the one who enjoyed exploring every enchanting nook and cranny, just as she had at Fittledale Park.

A small stab of nostalgia speared her, and she tightened her mouth for a pace.

She missed Fittledale Park, the quiet country estate near Colchester that Everleigh had purchased after her first husband's death. In point of fact, Rayne found nearly everything about London overwhelming: the routs, balls, soirees, musicals, the theater...*the men.*

Mostly the men.

She'd never completely outgrown her fear of males and, truth be told, doubted she ever would.

Although outings to Hyde Park, Green Park, and St. James' Park were enjoyable, one never knew how many acquaintances one might encounter. And worse, be forced to discuss trivial drivel with them. Unless she were atop a horse. When riding, Rayne could gallop Rotten Row and not have to partake in the usual boring twaddle.

And then there were the never-ending assemblies...

Well, honestly. They were nothing short of a perpetual competition to see who was the first tulip of fashion; who would dance with whom; who might make a brilliant match this Season; who might give someone the cut; and what succulent gossip might be spread about with the ease of whipped butter on a fresh-from-the-oven hot cross bun.

Rayne peered ahead to where the path ended near a pink tea rose-smothered arbor set before a stunning octagon cobalt-blue, sea-green, lavender, and white tile mosaic. An ostentatious sundial in the mosaic's center commanded one's attention, much like a grand dame entering a salon or prima donna upon the stage.

Impressive and impossible to ignore.

Her musings returned to the mysterious stairs. Surely Fitzroy, if no one else, must be aware of the unusual wall separating the properties. If Griffin didn't know the wall's history, mayhap the gardener did.

Fitzroy had come with the manor. Griffin had often said, "I don't think there is any question of him retiring to the country."

The charming rock expanse ran parallel to a tall, well-maintained hedgerow. So conceivably, the gardener hadn't given it much thought. There wasn't much reason to because no one occupied 19 Belford Square—the house next door.

That was rather unfortunate since the place was quite charming, in a lonely sort of way. As if it pined for its owners to return and fill it with life and love once more.

Nevertheless, the slightly overgrown gardens were something to behold. Whoever had designed them had possessed quite the artistic eye.

As meticulous and attractive as Fitzroy kept the Sheffields' grounds, the unkempt, natural beauty of the property next door beckoned Rayne as it had since she'd accidentally discovered it when she'd come to live in London after Aunt Everleigh had married Griffin.

In truth, Everleigh wasn't really Rayne's aunt.

Well, she was her step-aunt by marriage, but they shared no blood.

Such trivialities didn't matter to either of them. The women had grown as close as sisters while Everleigh had been married to Rayne's grand-uncle, Arnold Chatterton. Arnold had been estranged from his sister for many years and was a stranger to Rayne. Nevertheless, Grandmother's brother had been appointed her guardian when Mama and Grandma had died from influenza within a week of one another.

Now there had been an evil, *evil* man, as had been Arnold's equally depraved son, Frederick. Both spawns of Satan and now likely—*and deservedly*—warmed hell's deepest bowels.

A shiver scuttled down Rayne's spine and lifted the flesh along her arms. Her earlier joy evaporated with the alacrity of a water droplet sprinkled upon a roaring fire, taking her cheerful smile with it.

How very different Griffin was from Arnold and Frederick, thank God.

Even so, Rayne didn't doubt memories yet haunted Everleigh as much as they did her from the time they'd spent under Arnold and Frederick Chatterton's cruel thumbs. At thirteen, Rayne had gone to live at Keighsdon Hall and had endured their vindictiveness several years longer than Everleigh.

It had been a tumultuous, terrifying existence.

With a determined shake of her head, Rayne pushed those morose musings away and focused on the present.

Everleigh and Griffin intended to visit his lace and textile manufacturing plants today, which meant Rayne had hours to enjoy herself in the wild tangle next door. If all went well, she'd be home—her hair properly piled atop her head in the manner of every respectable young miss on the Marriage Mart—and possessing sketches that she might later create watercolors from, well before they returned.

As she reached the stone barrier, she took up her song once more.

"In June there was a yellow rosebud..."

Singing beneath her breath, she balanced her basket atop the wall's slightly rounded top. Once she'd gathered her skirts in one hand, she ascended the narrow steps, using the wall for balance. After carefully turning around, she descended the other side.

"And that is the flow'r for me."

"And that is...hmm, hmm, hmm."

Still humming, she'd hopped onto the slightly damp, shaded ground. Angling her face upward, she shook her hair so that it tumbled down her back.

I should've at least tied it back with a ribbon.

Oh well. Too late now.

Her mind already moving to the pleasant mission she'd set herself, Rayne collected her basket. Today she meant to draw the glorious wisteria—a task that would strain her humble artistic talents. She didn't draw for praise or recognition.

No, she sketched because she enjoyed trying to capture moments in time.

Everything she knew about drawing and painting had been self-taught, mostly while living at Keighsdon Hall. She had to do something with her time. Lonely, neglected, and an obvious inconvenience—Uncle Arnold hadn't even bothered with a governess after she'd turned fifteen—Rayne had learned to entertain herself.

The wisteria vine had escaped its staid arbor's confines and had twisted and entwined itself up a plane tree, creating an enchanting, fairly-like effect. The usually unremarkable tree appeared to be festooned with streaming purple flowers.

The result was quite stunning. Almost magical.

No properly attended garden would ever be permitted something so unrestrained and beautiful. A shame, really.

Why must everything be constrained by someone else's strictures and dictates of appropriateness, acceptability, or propriety?

Wasn't there any room for originality and uniqueness?

No. That was the unfortunate, undeniable, if somewhat unpleasant truth.

With a slight shrug for what she was powerless to change, Rayne took up singing where'd she left off.

"I oftentimes have pluck'd that yellow rosebud..."

"Wasna it a red rosebud?" an amused male inquired in a deep, melodious brogue.

Made in United States
North Haven, CT
15 November 2022